HAVEN OF THE HUNTED

HAVEN OF THE HUNTED

T. V. Olsen

Chivers Press • G.K. Hall & Co.
Bath, England • Thorndike, Maine USA

This Large Print edition is published by Chivers Press, England, and by
G.K. Hall & Co., USA.

Published in 1999 in the U.K. by arrangement with Golden West Literary
Agency.

Published in 1999 in the U.S. by arrangement with Golden West Literary
Agency.

U.K. Hardcover   ISBN 0-7540-3838-6   (Chivers Large Print)
U.K. Softcover   ISBN 0-7540-3839-4   (Camden Large Print)
U.S. Softcover   ISBN 0-7838-8649-7   (Nightingale Series Edition)

The text of this Large Print edition is unabridged.
Other aspects of the book may vary from the original edition.

Set in 16 pt. New Times Roman.

Printed in Great Britain on acid-free paper.

British Library Cataloguing in Publication Data available

Library of Congress Cataloging-in-Publication Data

Olsen, Theodore V.
    Haven of the hunted / T.V. Olsen.
       p.   cm.
    ISBN 0-7838-8649-7 (lg. print : sc : alk. paper)
    1. Large type books.   I. Title.
    [PS3565.L8H38 1999]
    813'.54—dc21   99–29285

CHAPTER ONE

Lute Danning, watching from the fly-blown front window of Red Rhuba's saloon, was the first to see the giant stranger riding into Dry Springs about sunset. Lute felt the stir of mounting excitement as he watched the man step from the saddle and tie his saddle horse to the tie-rail in front of Rhuba's. From the back of his packhorse, he untied an empty tarp.

The stranger ducked under the tie-rail, the tarp folded under his arm, and crossed the single shallow-rutted street, flanked by its tar-paper shacks, to McNamara's general store. As he stepped up on the boardwalk to enter McNamara's, the massive-shouldered, square-framed height of him was straight and erect in the fading light, and Lute had his moment of fleeting doubt. He's bigger than I remember, Lute thought. A lot bigger. But it had been since before the war ended that he'd last seen Doug Kingdom, and Kingdom had been only seventeen, perhaps, less, then.

Lute walked back to the bar and ordered a bottle of whiskey which he carried back to the table by the front window, from which he could command a view of the whole street. Lute shifted his fat short bulk restlessly and poured a glassful of whiskey, downing it.

Afterward, he tilted his dirty horsethief hat

1

to the back of his balding sandy-haired head and reflected bleakly on the two years that had fallen since the end of the war, when with others of Quantrell's guerrilla band he had attempted to surrender to United States troops only to be driven back with gunfire—to outlawry. The ruthlessness of Quantrell and of Bloody Bill Anderson was still a live and fearful thing in '65, the debacle of Lawrence, Kansas, in '63, a fresh horror in the minds of North and South alike.

Too early in '65 to forget how Quantrell had scourged borderline towns of Northern sympathizers and rebels alike, burning, looting, and murdering, regardless of the codes of warfare. And when Appomattox came, the legacy of hatred and fear that the guerrillas had reaped turned back on them and drove them to lair like hunted beasts, sport for the guns of Yankee patrols. The broken remnants of Quantrell's raiders were scattered; some, like Jesse and Frank James and like Lute Danning and like Doug Kingdom, to become wanted men west of the Missouri as well as east of it . . .

Lute broke from his gray musing as Kingdom stepped out the doorway of McNamara's, the tarp, bulging slightly with a slender quota of supplies, slung over a shoulder. He moved back across the road. With the heavy, dragfooted gait of a man too long in the saddle, he walked to the tie-rail and surveyed it briefly, gaunt face expressionless. For a moment he stood that way, motionless, and then Lute saw why. Kingdom's two horses, which he'd hitched there a few minutes before, were gone . . .

From his position at the table by Rhuba's front window, Lute saw that DeRoso was standing on Rhuba's boardwalk, his narrow, gangling-jointed frame loosely erect as he leaned with one shoulder against a gallery-supporting pillar. DeRoso was seventeen, pimply-faced, and straw-haired, with a Colt's .44 strapped ostentatiously low against the thigh of his frayed butternut-striped trousers. Lute also noticed Kingdom's gaze raking up and across the walk, settling upon DeRoso.

Kingdom studied the boy briefly, then said mildly, 'Where's my horses?'

DeRoso said blandly, 'What horses?'

Their voices carried plainly to Lute through the open door. He saw Kingdom's obsidian gaze flatten—then grow seemingly blacker with the acceptance of an irrevocable something. Only Kingdom's voice as he spoke, still watching DeRoso, held a fathomless patience. 'I'm going in for a drink.'

'Maybe you'll find them in the bottom of your glass,' DeRoso said slyly. Damn him! Lute thought.

Kingdom's face did not alter. He said gently, 'I will be out in five minutes. If they're not here, you'd better not be.'

3

Before DeRoso could say anything more, Kingdom had stepped up past him and through Rhuba's doorway. Kingdom paused briefly on the doorsill, his massive upper frame blocking the door space entirely, and eased the tarpful of supplies to the floor against the wall. Then he had his look around the room, his gaze settling with brevity on Lute by the window and moving to Red Rhuba behind the rough bar paralleling the right wall of the small room. Kingdom walked ponderously over to it, and Red ceased the dumping of dirty glasses in a hogshead half full of water of a dubitable gray cast, and put his big freckled hands on the bar. He was a stocky loose-jointed young man with a heavy flame-red thatch of hair falling in a great cowlick over his forehead. His kindly blue eyes regarded Kingdom questioningly.

'Whiskey,' Kingdom said. 'I'll take the bottle.'

Red set a bottle of Mountain Brook and a glass before him, said cheerfully, 'Count your own drinks,' and returned to the glasses.

Kingdom carried bottle and glass over to the farthest table by the wall, toed out a chair and slacked into it, morosely pouring a drink; and Lute, who was watching him from the side, covertly studied him now in rising puzzlement.

His face was weathered to a deep mahogany where a week's ink-black beard stubble did not sworl it into rough obscurity, a face which

4

seemed to have aged far beyond what was warranted by the three years since the war, Lute reflected. Yet it was the face of Doug Kingdom as Lute remembered it, to the deep-socketed obsidian eyes and the high-bridged nose. But the greatest physical inconsistency was the man's size. Doug was always big and strong, but his strength had been channeled into an intense nervous energy, barely restrained. This man was built like a blacksmith, big with a bigness that was all over, though with an unproportional concentration of weight through chest and shoulders. Yet this could be the added development of maturity, and much of his apparent height an illusion caused by his great breadth.

He carried no gun, and Lute marked that as strange, strange for Doug Kingdom . . . He was wearing a calico shirt, a black Stetson, wear-cracked boots, and blue army trousers, rusty with age, with the canary-yellow stripe of the United States Cavalry down the outseams. Lute noted in particular the trousers, and he noted too the mild amusement that briefly relaxed the man's straight mouth as he observed the fly-specked chromo of J. E. B. Stuart which hung over the backwall behind the bar. A Yankee? Lute wondered; yet the man's summer-soft voice when he'd spoken to Rhuba was distinctly Doug Kingdom's voice with its Tennessee backwoods drawl.

Lute's round cherub's face was beginning to

show his troubled confusion, and when Kingdom glanced up suddenly to see Lute still regarding him fixedly, Lute looked down, blushing. He reached for his drink, downed it, and began to rise to walk over to Kingdom, then slacked back into his chair.

Don't be a damn fool, Lute thought in self-disgust, and had again put his hands on the table to rise when DeRoso slouched in through the doorway and started toward the bar. Lute tried to catch his eye with a warning glare; DeRoso didn't notice or pretended not to. He bellied up to the bar, his gun butt banging loudly against it, and Red looked up from stacking glasses beneath the bar.

'Whiskey,' DeRoso said, 'and I'll take the bottle.'

Red deliberately finished stacking the glasses, and Lute saw the stir of anger in DeRoso's face. Lute realized that DeRoso's words were exactly the words Kingdom had used, that DeRoso was not yet through baiting the big man, and that Red saw it too.

DeRoso stopped in front of Kingdom's table, bottle in one hand and glass in the other. Kingdom looked up from his own glass, his expression—one of no bitterness, only deep, deep patience—not changing at the sight of DeRoso's mocking, reckless face.

'Want a drink?' asked DeRoso.

'I've got one,' Kingdom said. 'Did you fetch the horses?'

'Mind if I sit down?'

'There's other tables. Did you fetch my horses?'

DeRoso studied him a moment. 'It's good whiskey,' he said, extending his bottle toward Kingdom.

Kingdom leisurely slouched back in his chair, lifting one leg and doubling it, so that he could rest the heel on the edge of his chair, and Lute thought resignedly, here it comes.

Kingdom said pleasantly, 'You might ask the bartender to loan you his towel.'

DeRoso set his bottle gently on the table, scowling. 'What for?'

Kingdom said, still pleasantly, 'To wipe behind your ears. They need drying.'

Lute watched them, powerless to stop what happened. He saw the swift, pale fury lash DeRoso's face to violence as he dropped the glass, saw the downward slash of hand toward holstered Colt. As he grasped the gun, Kingdom's foot raised from the chair and drove savagely into the rim of the table top, so that it skittered violently into DeRoso; a shout of pain was driven from him as it pinned his hand against his gun butt, numbing the hand beyond use.

Kingdom was on his feet, skirting the table in two strides and doubling up the front of DeRoso's greasy buckskin shirt in his massive left fist while his right palm slapped DeRoso twice with cracking reports, and on the second

7

slap Kingdom let go of him, so that the blow staggered him backward the width of the small room, half stunned and fighting for balance. He lost it and fell heavily on his back by Lute's table.

From his back DeRoso clawed awkwardly for his gun with his left hand, and as he pulled it and was dragging it to a level, Lute came out of his chair. He took just one long step to bring his heel down on DeRoso's wrist, driving it to the floor, grinding down once, savagely, so that DeRoso's fingers splayed out with the pain of it, and his hold on the gun was gone.

Lute bent down, angrily jerked DeRoso to his feet by his shirt front, and booted him toward the doorway. DeRoso caught feebly at the doorjamb in passing, but his numbed fingers were unable to gain purchase and he tripped over the doorsill and fell to one knee on the walk. He came upright, whirling to face Lute. He was shaking with rage, his yellow eyes hot and savage with it. He said in nearly a whisper, 'Don't ever do that to me, Lute.'

Lute slapped him across the face, crowded him up hard against the saloon wall, DeRoso's collar doubled up in both hands. 'Know who you were salty with?' Lute snarled.

'Let go, damn you!'

'That was Doug Kingdom, friend.'

DeRoso's jaw went slack with surprise, and Lute, seeing it, slowly relaxed his hold.

'Kingdom,' DeRoso said in a dazed way.

'That's Doug Kingdom you told me about? One with you and Quantrell . . . ?'

'Him.'

DeRoso's hands shook as he straightened his shirt. He said, 'My God. He could of killed me.'

'I wish to hell he had,' Lute said bitterly. 'Good God, do I always have to change your diapers? Who talked you off the day that Red River bunch was going to hang you for brand-blotting?'

'You did,' DeRoso said sullenly.

'Who else would of stepped for you that time the Dallas gambler was going to shoot you for cold-decking him?'

'No one,' DeRoso said sullenly.

'And I expect to be leveled with. Walk soft around Kingdom; else, don't walk. Or he'll fix you so you won't.' Lute paused. 'Where's his horses?'

DeRoso didn't reply for a moment, regarding the ground surlily. Then he said, 'Around back of the saloon.'

'Bring 'em back here,' Lute said flatly, and without another word turned and stalked back into Rhuba's, pausing by his table to pick up DeRoso's gun. As Lute straightened he saw that Red had laid a shotgun across the bar and was leaning his elbows on the bar, silently watching him.

'This ain't Dallas,' Red said finally.

'You won't have no more trouble off him,

9

Red,' Lute said mildly.

Red musingly dropped his gaze to his shotgun. 'That's right, Lute,' he agreed negligently.

Lute glanced at Kingdom, and seeing that Kingdom was watching him steadily, walked stiffly over to the table. 'Long time, Kingdom,' Lute said, and watched the mild shock of astonishment at being called by name wash across Kingdom's passive face. The doubts, the suspicions, tided back on Lute, and he thought cautiously, Play it cozy.

He waited, watching Kingdom's face with care, seeing the immobility veil it again. 'Long enough,' Kingdom said.

'You remember me?' Lute said doubtfully. 'Lute Danning? With Quantrell . . .'

'Sure,' Kingdom said. 'Sure, I remember you.'

He nodded toward the chair opposite him. Lute pulled it up and eased into it, now as always, choosing his words. 'You didn't get my note up north, Doug—Dallas?'

And this time Lute could have sworn the man gave a visible start; yet Kingdom's dark and withdrawn face was so placid he must have been mistaken . . . Odd, in Doug—this colorless reserve . . .

'I passed through Dallas on the run,' Kingdom said idly. 'The marshal had me move. I was an unsavory influence.'

Lute said, 'You would be,' with a grin. He

10

felt relief. This explained Kingdom's surprise and his first lack of recognition. He had come to Dry Springs by chance, not following the note.

'This note,' Lute added, 'I left it with the apron at the Chuckaway saloon there. Told me you always came there when in Dallas.'

Kingdom poured another whiskey, but didn't down it. He sat broodingly turning the glass between his hands, speculatively regarding it. 'You were looking for me, then.'

'In every trail town from the Trinity to the Nueces. You were in that range somewhere; that was all I knew.'

Kingdom sipped his drink. 'You must have wanted to see me some.'

'For a year now. You have a hell of a rep in this part of the world, fella.'

'Do I now,' Kingdom murmured. 'And how are you thinking of using it?'

Lute blushed at the accuracy of this. He removed his horsethief hat and laid it on the table at his elbow, then leaned across the table in a confidential manner. 'We can use each other, Doug.' His merry little eyes were watchful and excited. Upon Kingdom's reply hinged his whole plan.

'Go on,' Kingdom said, and then Lute saw his eyes shift to the door, which was at Lute's back. Because he was not usually so lax as to leave his back open, Lute mentally cursed his own carelessness as he swiftly turned in his

11

seat. DeRoso was standing in the doorway, sullenly watching them.

'You put them horses back?' Lute demanded.

DeRoso nodded and stepped over to the table where his bottle of whiskey still stood; he picked it up by the neck and took a massive slug, squinting against the raw sting of it.

Kingdom stood up, nodding to Lute. 'Obliged. I'll put my horses up, then come back and talk this over. There a livery or feed barn around?'

'On the south end of town, first building to your right as you ride out,' Lute said. His voice was affable though he inwardly felt a sour irritation at this delay.

Kingdom nodded his thanks and walked over to the bar to pay Red, then strode out. Lute morosely reached for Kingdom's empty glass, poured it full, and tossed it down.

'He going in with us?' DeRoso asked.

'I don't know yet.'

Lute noticed only now that darkness had settled over the town. Red lighted a wall lamp at either end of the bar. The murky saffron light burned in a sickly way to the corners of the room. Two drifters came in and bellied against the bar. Lute was facing the door, staring at the floor, when he heard the ring of a spur on the doorsill and looked up to see Kingdom standing there in the doorway.

Lute's face whitened; the glass in his hand

shattered on the floor. 'Huh?' said DeRoso.

Kingdom? Doug? Lute thought wildly.

This man was wearing faded levis and a tattered jumper and wore a gun. His face was that of the man to whom Lute had been speaking, but it was younger, holding an irrepressible gaiety in it. He was big, but still shorter and much lighter than the man in the rusty blue army trousers; and now as his face turned toward Lute, Lute saw the pleased recognition in the bone-white smile that flashed on the instant his bright gaze fell on Lute . . .

And this was Doug Kingdom.

But the giant stranger? Lute, recalling his suspicions, sank back into his chair, his mind dull-blank with the terrified shock of this moment.

CHAPTER TWO

Doug Kingdom stepped forward, smiling, to grasp Lute's limp hand hard. 'Lute, you damn jayhawker! When your note said I'd find you in Dry Springs, I knew that meant the saloon in Dry Springs.'

DeRoso's mouth had slacked open in astonishment. He made a limp gesture at Doug and stared at Lute.

'You—got my note?' Lute said in a distant

13

voice. He wondered obscurely if it was his own.

'At the Chuckaway in Dallas, sure . . .' Doug glanced at DeRoso. 'Friend of yours?' Doug's real attention was on the bottle of whiskey, and he slacked into a chair and reached for the bottle and a glass.

'Yeah,' Lute said shakily. 'Fred DeRoso, Doug Kingdom.'

Doug barely nodded to DeRoso, drained a glass of whiskey, and set it down, wiping the palm of his hand across his mouth. 'Washes the trail down,' he observed. 'Let's get down to cases, Lute . . . What in hell's eating you?' Doug reached for the tobacco in his jumper pocket, looking curiously from Lute to DeRoso.

Lute said with difficulty, 'Fella came in a few minutes before you did.' He cleared his throat. 'Looked like you—said he was you . . .'

Doug's fingers froze in the shaping of a wheat-straw cigarette. Then he said slowly in a voice guttural with unnatural strain:

'Looked like me . . . ? How much like me?'

'Older than you—maybe ten years older . . .'

'But big—a lot bigger than me . . .'

'Built like an ox,' DeRoso said.

The makings fell unnoticed from Doug's fingers to the table; his deeply recessed eyes suddenly burned like live coals. He said in a trembling, almost inaudible voice, 'Knew he'd come some day. Ma Kingdom's pride and joy . . . Hell!'

14

Lute leaned forward, gripping the table in his intensity: 'Who? Who?'

Doug looked at him. Without seeing him, Lute thought eerily. 'My brother Jim. Big brother Jim. Yeah.' Doug squinted suddenly, almost painfully. 'Give me a drink, damn you . . .'

Lute silently handed him a bottle. Doug fumbled for it without looking at it; tilted it up and drained what remained in it nearly empty before he set it down. He placed his hands on the table to steady himself till he could regain his breath. DeRoso gave him a silent, respectful regard.

Doug looked now at Lute, saying in a normal voice: 'Where is he?'

'Went to put his horses up at the livery. Should have been back by now,' Lute said, glancing apprehensively at the door.

'He'll try to take me back. He'll try to make me give up to what he calls the law and pay for my—misdeeds. Well, he can got to hell,' Doug said softly. 'He can go to hell. I'm not going back . . . You hear me, Lute . . .?'

'Yeah,' Lute said, picking up his hat and jerking his head toward the door. Doug and DeRoso followed him out. They stepped along the narrow path worn through the rank weeds by the front wall of the building until they were a good talking distance from the bar; voices would carry far in the windless, still night. Lute paused then, turning to face Doug's dark form,

15

voicing the thought which had been in his mind:

'Him being your brother, you wouldn't shoot him . . .'

'How do you know I wouldn't?' Doug snapped out of the darkness. He paused then; a little drunk, Lute decided, and not altogether clear in his mind. Finally Doug said slowly, 'You're right: I wouldn't shoot him. And the Almighty help you if you try to . . .'

'Sure,' Lute murmured. 'But we have to get him out of our way. There's a way without hurting him—much.'

'How . . . ? I can't bluff him with a gun. He'll know I wouldn't shoot. Think I'd trust either of you to hold one on him, without shooting? Think again, Lute-boy.'

'Suppose we all jump him?' DeRoso put in.

'Hell, he could handle ten like us without trying,' Doug said softly.

'Still, there's a way,' Lute said insistently. 'He'll come back along this way from the livery to Rhuba's.'

'He would of left the livery by now,' said DeRoso. 'Must of gone to the cafe to eat.'

'Maybe not,' Doug said slowly. 'You don't know him . . . Likely to see to taking care of his horses himself.'

'Listen,' Lute said quickly. 'Fred and I'll get in this alley. You stay here on the walk. When your brother comes by, get his attention . . . I'll do the rest.'

16

'Watch it,' DeRoso whispered sharply. 'Someone coming from the livery now ...'

Two men stepped from the livery stable down the street, and Lute saw a distinct tremor run over Doug. One of the men, holding a bull's eye lantern, was the white-haired hostler; the other, towering in the lantern glow, Jim Kingdom.

Doug watched hungrily, briefly, the brother he had not seen in six years, then gave Lute a long and sultry glance: 'You tap him gentle, Lute, hear?'

'Sure, sure,' Lute said irritably; he caught DeRoso by the arm and pulled him into the narrow, shadowed alley.

Lute waited, crouching against a wall.

Sweat broke on his face—he had forgotten he'd left his gun in his room. He heard DeRoso's hollow stertorous breathing behind him, and he reached a hand back into the darkness; it touched DeRoso's greasy shirt.

Lute whispered sharply, 'Give me your gun,' and waited till he felt it shoved into his hand. He wondered whether to grasp it by the butt or barrel for the blow, and decided that the stock would afford a more certain grip.

Lute could see the black hulk of Doug on the walk, leaning negligently against the building. Then Lute heard the booted steps of a heavy man crunching along the walk.

He heard Doug call softly, 'Jim,' just as the big man stepped past the mouth of the alley.

He saw Jim come to a dead stop, leaning as though to discern the face of the man who spoke, and it was now that Lute moved one step forward, swinging his pistol savagely at the back of Jim's uncovered head. In the uncertain light, he nearly missed, and the heavy barrel of the .44 hit the big man only a glancing blow that staggered him, and brought him into a half turn as though to face his assailant.

Lute struck again, wildly, and the muzzle hit Jim Kingdom solidly over the temple. Kingdom's knees hinged and he fell forward. Doug had already moved to catch him as he fell; his brother's great weight dragged him down too.

Doug whispered, 'Help me with him, Lute, damn you!'

'Where can we take him?' DeRoso asked hoarsely.

Lute handed DeRoso the gun and bent down to catch Jim around the legs, grunting with the effort as he and Doug lifted him between them. 'My room—across the street—back of the store—Anyone coming—Fred?'

'Street's clear,' DeRoso said.

Lute and Doug carried the unconscious man between them, across the deserted street and down the wide alley between a rooming house and a keno parlor. They skirted to the rear of the buildings. Once Doug swore as he tripped over a bucket and nearly fell. Guided mainly by the familiarity of association, Lute found his way in the moonless night to the very door of the tar-paper lean-to he lived in at the rear of McNamara's store.

'Set him down,' Lute said breathlessly, 'till I find the lamp . . .'

He eased Jim's feet to the ground and opened the door. In the dark room, he located the lamp on the commode by the left wall. He struck a match, lighted it, and replaced the chimney. Light flickered uncertainly about the room. Besides the battered commode, the room was meagerly furnished with a straw tick on the rough-plank floor, just by the door, on which Lute had spread his bedroll. He and Doug lifted Jim inside and lowered him onto the bedroll.

Doug went down on his knees by Jim and parted his thick black hair over the temple where Lute's gun had struck the second time. The skin was split, blood already thinly matting the hair. Doug glanced at Lute, his face gone white and bitter, his eyes like molten obsidian. He said suddenly, hotly, 'I ought to shoot you, Lute.'

Lute's own nerves were keyed to a breaking pitch. He said harshly, 'Did you think of any other way?' He rubbed his aching arms.

Doug stood up slowly, his gaunt face drawn into a tired resignation. 'I'm sorry, Lute,' he said wearily. 'I can't stand to see anyone hurt him at all.' He met Lute's gaze fixedly. 'You

19

want to understand that, Lute—anyone . . .'

'Sure,' Lute said, 'sure.' He looked back at the fallen man, and when he spoke, it was with hesitance because of his uncertainty of Doug's temper. 'If you don't want to hold a gun on him, we better tie him before he comes out of it . . .'

'*I'll* do it,' Doug snapped. 'Any rope?'

Under his straw tick, Lute located some long strands of rawhide for a riata which he had never gotten around to braiding. Doug tied his brother tightly hand and foot—the hands in front for comfort. DeRoso opened his mouth to protest this; Lute shot him a warning glance. Doug straightened to his feet now and began restlessly to shape a cigarette.

'Just why you want to see me, Lute?'

Lute set his back comfortably to the wall. 'You've made yourself a reputation in the trail towns since you reached Texas . . .'

Doug made a wry face. 'And all bad. That have anything to do with it?'

'Everything to do with it,' Lute said flatly. He was silent for a moment. Long ago he had planned what he would say to Doug when they met, and now he silently reviewed it before he spoke. 'Kid, you're footloose. I'm footloose. We're both wanted. We've been running a long time, sleeping with one eye open and facing doors and windows and pulling penny-ante jobs for eats . . .'

Doug regarded him quizzically. 'Didn't

20

know you were in Texas till I got that note in Dallas. You been living the hard way too?'

'I have,' Lute growled, 'and I'm damn well tired of it. After Bloody Bill and George Todd ran Quantrell out of Missouri, I left too. The outfit was falling to pieces. I lone-wolfed it since, but that's no good either. With Quantrell, there was at least safety in numbers . . . You stuck with Todd, didn't you?'

'Till he was killed at the Little Blue,' Doug said wearily. 'Now will you spit the meal out of your mouth, Lute?'

Lute was about to speak when the unconscious man moaned softly and stirred on Lute's bedroll. Doug threw his unlighted cigarette away; he stooped beside his brother.

Jim Kingdom's eyes opened then; he lifted his head, squinting painfully against the light. He tried to move his arms and legs, and, seeing that they were tied, contented himself with swinging up to a sitting position, wincing at the pain it caused him. Seeing Doug squatting before him, he did not smile. Doug did, not very heartily:

'You made your loop too big, General.'

'That happens,' Jim murmured. His dark eyes shifted a little, and settled on Lute and then DeRoso. 'So this is what you have taken to running with . . .'

Doug stood up. He said dryly, 'Did you come all the way from Tennessee to tell me that?'

21

'I didn't come to tell you anything,' Jim said sparely. 'Ma told me to find and see you're all right. I intend to.'

'Well, you saw me—I'm all right.'

Jim looked at him; he laughed softly; then, with an effort raised his upper body from the blankets, his lips tight against his bared teeth in a noiseless grimace. The movement caused a livid trickle of blood down the side of his face. 'Fool,' he said quietly. 'You're all wrong.'

Doug paced across the room, slowly, and back. A soft, almost hidden pain worked soundlessly in his face. 'How is Ma?'

'She's dead,' Jim Kingdom said in an iron voice. 'Last thought was of you. Find Doug. She loved you, damn you, more than any of us; more than me, Pa, or Polly or Jo or Jubal— more than any of us ... You never gave a damn, though, did you?' He cruelly ignored the agony in Doug's face. 'You killed her, sure as a bullet. You who couldn't come home because Pa would have killed you, knowing what he did about you; how you rode with Quantrell and burned homes and murdered women and children—you—oh, damn you to hell!'

'Stop it!' Doug shouted savagely, then wheeled at the sharp metallic cocking of DeRoso's .44.

'I'll stop him,' DeRoso suggested.

Doug did not hesitate; he took two steps to DeRoso and hit him in the face. DeRoso

22

stumbled backward, crashing into the commode. He swayed there a moment, his face blank; then the hatred took it fully, and his gun came to a level on Doug's chest.

'Fred!'

The whiplash of Lute's voice somehow broke through DeRoso's rage. He swayed on his feet, his gun held rigid before him for a long instant in which Lute did not breathe at all; then the muzzle slacked, slowly. Doug eased his half-drawn gun back into its holster. Lute breathed again; he came erect and stalked to the commode, yanking it open. He pulled out a dragoon gun and belt and strapped it on.

Lute slapped it and looked at them. 'I'll take no more,' he said grimly. 'Not off either of you.'

'Don't threaten me, Lute,' Doug said mildly, not impressed. 'Just keep the kid away from me. He stinks.' He swung back to his brother.

DeRoso turned white, a hellish fury in his pale eyes, but he was wholly in check now, any impulse further governed by the plain warning in Lute's face.

Doug was saying, 'General, this is no place for you. You go home to the old man. I let you go, promise that.'

'You know the answer.'

Doug said patiently, 'This's getting us exactly nowhere. Fella, I can't go back. The old man would shoot me himself; you said so ...

What else is there for me?'

Jim looked at him fully. 'You can pay up,' he said flatly.

'Pay what? I got nothing to pay except my life. And that would rot away in a federal prison. Quantrell—'

'Appomattox was two years ago,' Jim said savagely. 'I mean since. Go off somewhere, change your name. But go on like this and you're lost.'

Doug said in a tried and patient way, 'Three years of this mark a man. No matter how far you go, you can't turn back . . . Only you quit this damn foolishness and go home.'

'No.'

Lute said uneasily, 'What are we going to do with him?'

Doug regarded Lute flatly and without compromise. 'Don't know, Lute. Know what we're *not* going to do, put it that way . . . Go on with what you were telling me.'

Lute glanced at Doug's brother.

'What's the difference?' Doug said irritably. 'If he was posing as me, he knows you're up to something . . .'

Lute hesitated for an unhappy moment and nodded uncomfortably. 'It's this, Doug. There's safety in numbers. Money, too. Bunch of us organize, we could strike back instead of running. Get some real loot into the bargain.' He paused.

Doug said dryly, 'I'm listening.'

'You remember when we were with Quantrell—the James boys, Frank, Jesse? And Cole Younger? After the war they organized. Men like us. Paid off. Can for us.'

Doug said skeptically, 'How do we get these—men like us . . . ?'

Lute smiled meagerly. 'I haven't just been riding back and forth across Texas to look for you. I've talked to men in dozens of towns and on the trail. Ex-rebs, ex-yanks. Spicks, breeds, men from fifteen to fifty. A lot of them think I got something. Small bunch of hard-riding men can do more for themselves than a hundred times that number sifted through the state.'

'For instance . . .'

'Planned bank and train robberies. Jayhawking cattle. A herd is gold on the hoof these days . . . Besides—I've got a system, Doug. Yes, a real system . . .'

'Why you looking for me in particular though?'

'We'll need a leader,' Lute said mildly, and watched the astonishment wash thinly across Doug's face.

'Me.'

Lute nodded somberly.

'Your idea,' Doug pointed out dryly. 'Why not you?'

'Unh-uh. I can plan and I can organize, but I'm fat and I'm too cautious. I'm a slow thinker and I'm getting on the wrong side of thirty. That's young for anything else, but not for this.'

'Put it this way, then,' Doug said. 'Why me?'

'For opposite reasons. Nerves, youth, fast as I'm not. You got the knack for handling men. Seen that back with Quantrell. These hard-cases know who you are, they'll toe the line. Don't know another who could handle them, see . . . ?'

Doug removed his hat thoughtfully and musingly fingered the frayed brim. 'You say you have the men lined up.'

Lute nodded. 'We'll move around—pick 'em up on the quiet . . .'

Doug glanced idly at DeRoso. 'He an example?'

A glance at DeRoso's face told Lute that DeRoso would have to go; he and Doug wouldn't mix.

'Listen to me, Doug,' Jim Kingdom said coldly. 'You're on the borderline now. Only start raking this fat boy's chestnuts out of the fire by letting him use your name as the head of this scum he's pulling together, you'll be a target for every man who recognizes you.'

'Sorry, General . . . What the man says makes sense. I'm tired of being told to move on . . .' Doug watched his brother, briefly, sadly, then clamped his hat on tightly and moved toward the door. 'We're riding out now. You make enough noise after we're gone and someone will find you. Only don't follow us.'

DeRoso was standing at the far end of the room by the battered commode and he said now, his face a malignant saffron mask in the lamplight, 'On the quiet, Lute, you said ... How's that tally with letting Big Brother go so he can tell every law in the country? We'll be broken before we're started ...'

Doug stopped. He said flatly, 'You won't be along to worry about it. Damn if I'll have a trigger-happy sheepherder's pup after a fast rep dragging along for a chance to shoot me in the back.'

He wheeled, starting for the door again ...

Suddenly, goaded beyond patience, beyond fear, DeRoso pulled his gun and shouted, *'Turn, damn you, Kingdom!'*

The breaking pitch of DeRoso's voice brought Doug around, but barely touching his gun, when DeRoso shot. Doug buckled in the middle and came partly erect, still on his feet, to get his gun pulled, when DeRoso shot again. Doug was smashed back, dropping his gun and falling half through the open door.

DeRoso swung his weapon on Lute. 'You move, Lute, and I'll kill you!'

DeRoso's attention was pulled from the door; he didn't see that Jim Kingdom had already dragged himself to his knees and was working with a terrible concentration to keep his balance as he leaned forward to grasp Doug's fallen gun between his bound hands and maneuver it into one fist.

27

Jim Kingdom fired once. The rickety commode rocked with a shuddering crash against the wall as DeRoso was flung into it. DeRoso dropped to his knees, a blankness filming his eyes; he fought to lift his gun, failed, and fell on his face.

Lute was already diving for the doorway. His gun was out now, but even in the passion of the moment, he would not shoot at Doug's brother. Jim Kingdom, in a blind fury, shot at him as he reached the door and the slug missed by only inches, whirring like an angry hornet into the darkness.

He ran for the side of the building to cut around it to the street when he heard the pounding of footsteps on the boardwalk by Rhuba's. The shots, he thought, and veered away from the street, cutting back from the building at right angles and into the concealment of the darkness beyond. He stopped abruptly, hunkering down in the tall grass, making himself small in the night as men rushed around the corner of the building and poured into the open doorway of Lute's room.

Lute heard the flurry of their voices as he squatted there in the sage, trying to think over the pounding of his heart. Everything he owned, except his horse and the clothes on his back, was in that room, and he would have to leave—now—without it. His horse was in the livery, but his saddle was in the room, and for one panicked moment he couldn't think

28

beyond that. He thought fleetingly of asking the hostler for the loan of a saddle and bridle and rejected this thought as it came. There would be questions for which he was too unnerved to conjure answers . . .

Then he recalled that when he and DeRoso and Doug had left Rhuba's, Doug's stud sorrel had been hitched to the tie-rail. Lute could safely assume that the shots had by now drawn everyone off the street . . .

Instantly, with fresh hope, he came to his feet and, skirting the building widely, started at a run for the street. The sorrel was there, he saw; and he slowed to a casual but hurried walk. He angled across the street by Rhuba's, coming up beside the horse and pausing there to cast a fleeting glance around. The saloon was empty and there was no one in sight on the street. He paused long enough to check the latigo, then took the reins and stepped into the saddle, wheeling the horse and starting him into a dead run downstreet.

It was a dark night, and once past the last building, Lute slowed down. There would be no pursuit at night, and he could make dry camp a little farther on; Doug's suggans were still lashed to his cantle.

Lute rode on, heading in a vaguely southerly direction, oddly dead to the passions that had driven him into the night, running again.

29

CHAPTER THREE

On his knees, Jim Kingdom strained his eyes into the sooty blackness beyond the door where Lute had disappeared, but presently, distinguishing no sign of the man, he slowly, with a great sigh, dropped the gun to the floor. His gaze fell to Doug, sprawled across the threshold. The crazed fury of seeing his brother shot down before his eyes evaporated into a deadness that left him drained and tired beyond thought.

The rush of feet outside brought him to his senses, and several men came in; the first was Red Rhuba, in his soiled bar apron and carrying his shotgun in one big freckled fist. His blue eyes took in the scene in one scanning glance—two fallen men and Jim Kingdom on his knees tied hand and foot.

'Hell,' Red said feelingly. 'What happened, friend?' He saw the residue of blank shock in Jim's face, and saw that the big man was looking at him without seeing him.

Red cut Jim loose and helped him up. Silently Jim moved to his brother's side and went down on one knee beside him. The first bullet had hit Doug low above the groin; Jim could feel Doug's own pain as he watched his brother's eyes flick open. His lips parted, touched now with a thin lacing of bloody foam.

30

Punctured lung, Jim thought, and something sank and died in him.

Doug recognized him and tried to speak, barely succeeding. 'Different story with an even break, General . . .'

'I got him, Doug.'

'You? There's a hero.' He actually smiled. 'Funny, can't lift my head. No feeling. A hell of a way to . . .'

'Doug—'

'No, listen.' His breath shortened. ' . . . There's a girl. I married her. Melanie Hassard.' He caught Jim's arm. 'Runs rooming house—town of Boundary. Due south to Rio Grande. Tell her—tell Melanie—I'm sorry. Just tell her that . . . Sorry . . .' He squinted. 'Fella, you there?'

'Yes, Doug.'

'Yes. Funny—I thought . . . Go home. Tell the old man—tell—' His voice trailed into a racking cough; he looked at Jim. It was odd, very very odd, how suddenly clear-eyed he was, with that sly gleam of well-remembered humor . . . 'You tell the old man I said to go to hell. He'll believe that—he'll believe—believe . . .'

It was ended. Ended so imperceptibly that it was a moment before Jim fully realized it. Only the sly humor had gone to leave the eyes varnished with blankness, and there was no more talk and there was no more coughing; and Kingdom lifted the body of his brother

31

very gently in his arms and turned to face those who stood in the room watching him silently, expectantly; and he looked at them still without seeing them. Carrying his brother, he stepped noiselessly out the door and into the shadowed and formless night.

'All right, boys,' he heard Rhuba say. 'Get on back. Drinks on the house. It's all over . . .'

Jim Kingdom, staring into the cobalt void of the night, vaguely heard the murmuring of the men leaving the leanto. Yes, Kingdom said silently; yes, it's all over . . .

He heard footsteps behind him and was presently aware that Red Rhuba had come to stand beside him. 'There's a cleared spot back of my place we use for burying,' Red said gently. He paused and cleared his throat. 'I got a shovel.'

Find him, Jim, Kingdom's mother had said. Find Doug and see he's all right.

Yes. Yes, Ma. He's all right. Doug's all right now. The rest of it doesn't matter. He's all right . . .

Jim roused a little. He looked at Red, trying to hold to Red's words over the throbbing ache of his head. At last he said in a dull, half-comprehending way, 'Yes. Thank you.'

*　　　*　　　*

Jim Kingdom rode out of Dry Springs before dawn.

The first thing was to find Melanie Hassard. Red had told him that Boundary lay due southwest; the simplest way to find the town was to strike west until he hit the stage route, perhaps three hours' ride, and follow it south to Boundary.

Jim reached the stage road before noon, and by noon had caught up with the stage when it stopped at Ocotillo Station. Here, at the direction of the driver, a small spare man of vinegar-waspish temper, he tied his horse behind the stage. Without waiting to eat, Kingdom climbed inside, settled onto a horsehair-padded seat, and, in a stuporous exhaustion of more than twenty-nine strenuous and sleepless hours, was asleep even before his glare-strained eyes could become accustomed to the subdued interior of the coach.

He scarcely realized that there were three other passengers until the jolting of the stage awakened him two hours later. A small tattered tramp, unwashed, unshaven, and unfriendly, sat beside Kingdom. The young man across from the tramp was not especially garrulous, merely hungry for talk; his name, he said, was Jean-Paul Villon. He and his wife were traveling from New Orleans to live on her father's ranch near Boundary.

Kingdom had met one or two Creoles during the war; this slender, frail young man of middle height he judged to be one, with his queued black hair and his soft-voiced accent. His slender expressive hands were completely graceful, completely aesthetic. He wore the tight fawn-colored trousers of the fashion of ten years before, a travel-grimed white sharkskin waistcoat, gold-embroidered, and a black frock coat. He had frequent and violent fits of coughing. In spite of his frailty and his quiet-seeming mien, there was an erect and fearless pride in his carriage that Kingdom found admirable in a man so little gifted physically, however handsome facially.

His wife was far less impressive at first glance; a small girl of good form but thinned down. She wasn't pretty; her mouth was too wide, her nose too short, and her eyebrows oddly sun-bleached so much lighter than her dark chestnut hair that they were nearly invisible against her pale skin. Yet her violet eyes held a childlike charm that seemed far from spurious, enhanced by the faint tracery of freckles across the bridge of her nose.

Character, Kingdom thought, was a poor and inadequate word for the compounding of pride and gentleness that he saw in this girl. Goodness was better. She was not yet twenty, he judged, though her husband was little under Kingdom's own age, which was thirty-one. Her dress was of plain calico with a short blue cape of better material and she wore both with a warm and human queenliness; but there was sweet and patient resignation in her face that

34

made Kingdom think. She could stand to laugh a little.

'My father-in-law used to ranch on the Louisiana side of the Sabine,' said Villon. 'He heard there was good grazing land by the Rio Grande so he sold out and established a ranch down here shortly before the war. He wrote us at New Orleans to come and live with him. I was doing well at my portrait painting in Orleans, but my physician insisted that the bayau country is bad for my lung condition. I was glad to accept the invitation. I am bringing my savings too, which are not inconsiderable. I hope to go into partnership in cattle with him. I have heard that the business has potentialities. From your experience in this part of the country, what would you say?'

Kingdom shrugged sparely. 'I only came West not long ago myself. Never been so far south as the Rio. Heard it's good for cattle. But cattle isn't always money.'

'What do you mean, sir?'

'Question of a market,' Kingdom said dryly. 'You have to get a herd to a shipping center. In Texas, that means a trail-drive hundreds of miles. Missouri, Louisiana. Indians, border gangs, flooded rivers, dry water holes every mile of the way. Lot of ranchers hate to try it; those that aren't have to sell their souls to get a crew with the insides to make the drive all the way. If they do get through, they're likely lucky to have enough cattle left to sell to pay

35

off the crew.'

'Is Missouri the best way?'

'That's what they said in Springfield. But there was talk of the railroad pushing west into Kansas.'

'Would a Kansas drive be better?'

'Couldn't say. There's bad country up through the Nations. You'd have to talk to—'

The entire coach seemed to half lift under the sudden violence of its braking; the shoes squealed savagely and trailed into silence as the stage rocked to a stop, creaking heavily back on the thorough braces. Kingdom pulled the leather dust curtains back and thrust his head from the window. Villon called in a shaken voice, 'What is it, Mr. Hollister?'

'What the hell you mean by riding at us like that? Want to get run down?' came the driver's angry-strident voice.

'Just take it easy,' the horseman said gently.

Kingdom could see the man now; he had reined close around to the side of the coach, a small young man in a baggy black suit. His smile was narrow and warning, yet the white flash of it was utterly good-natured and reckless; and mad flecks danced merrily in his black-irised eyes. The curly black hair, glossy as a cricket's shell, which tumbled carelessly from beneath his back-tilted gray hat, only heightened his uncaring air. His gaze moved to Kingdom looking from the window, and he smiled a little more and nodded cheerfully.

36

Hollister's voice softened and there was an almighty patience to it. 'Son, if you don't move off, so help me I'll knock you clean out of your saddle with this popper.'

The young man's heavy-lidded gaze moved almost idly away from Kingdom to the driver. 'Don't push it, grandpa,' he murmured, his smile gentle to the extreme. His slim hands were crossed negligently on the pommel . . .

Kingdom quietly drew Doug's revolver from the waist of his trousers and eased it up to the window, then stopped in the act of laying the long barrel across the sill. A fullsize dragoon revolver had appeared as if by magic in the stranger's slim hand. He held it loosely, but he smiled directly at Kingdom as he spoke.

'I wouldn't, friend. I really wouldn't. It wouldn't do, you know. You're a big man, but a little bullet could stop you dead. Quite dead.'

The youth reined his horse in nearer to the rear of the stage, grinning in at the passengers. He motioned with his gun, his attention on the others: 'Throw it out, friend.' Kingdom didn't move. The boy glanced at him, his voice softening a shade. 'Throw it out, friend.'

Kingdom let the gun drop out the window. The youth looked at Villon. 'Now. You.'

'I pack none,' Villon said with a stiff and outraged formality.

'You, then, grandpa. Both of them.' Hollister threw pistol and shotgun out in to the road; the bandit pulled in close to the stage door and leaned from his saddle to wrench it open. 'Out, my children. Sit tight on your whiskers up there, grandpa.'

Kingdom climbed out, helped Mrs. Villon to the ground, and gave Villon a hand down. Kingdom looked around then at the bandit.

'Throw your wallet up, friend. Reach for it slow . . . That's fine.'

Kingdom threw the bandit the worn leather sheaf and his free hand snaked it easily out of the air. Kingdom watched him take out the solitary gold eagle inside. It made a bright twinkle in the sunlight as he spun it into the air with a laugh, caught it, and slid it into the wallet. The stranger tossed it back with such fluid unexpectedness that it hit Kingdom in the chest before he caught it on the rebound.

'Buy yourself some champagne, friend,' the youth said merrily. He looked at the little tramp, Loomis, flicking a black lightning glance over him; he laughed. He motioned at Villon. 'All right—you.'

'I have nothing.'

'Untruths, untruths . . . ! Throw your coat up here. Then empty your pockets.'

He looked through Villon's coat, said 'Hm,' thoughtfully, and tossed it back. 'Come on, the other stuff.'

Villon passed up the articles from his pockets—cigar case, expensive gold watch case, and wallet. The youth examined the articles, looked in the fine Morocco wallet, then carelessly threw all three costly items back into the dust at Villon's feet.

'Nice, but not much compared to what you must be hiding somewhere,' he said musingly.

Villon had said he was bringing a large sum from New Orleans and it was obvious he would not carry a large sum in the open. His prosperous appearance was a giveaway, though.

'You, grandpa,' said the young man. 'Get down and get this pilgrim's luggage out.'

Hollister hauled all of Villon's bags out and opened and rifled through them at the youth's directions. At the end of this fruitless search, the bandit grinned and scratched his jaw, then looked idly at Mrs. Villon. 'Your wife . . . ?'

'Yes,' Villon said tensely.

The bandit's gaze moved down her, stopping at her waist. Instinctively, she half lifted a hand, then dropped it quickly. The highwayman smiled disarmingly, saying to Villon, 'Money belt. And on your wife rather than you. Clever.' He nodded to Villon's wife and waggled his gun barrel at her. 'All right, lady.'

She did not move; merely watched him without fear. 'But it's under my dress,' her voice not losing a jot of its soft calm.

A murderous rage blazed suddenly across Villon's face. '*Sacre!* You misbegotten beast! If you—'

The youth, some eager, savage impulse

breaking through his indifference, swiveled his gun to cover Villon. 'Want to say something?'

For a split second the naked urge to do murder danced madly through the youth's black eyes. Villon's mouth worked silently, then closed; his face was white, more with the pitifully angry knowledge of futility than fear.

The youth said, again mildly, 'Get in the coach, ma'am. All I want is the belt. Only be quick about it . . .'

Relief crossed Villon's face, but only for a moment. He said shortly, 'Don't do it, Wanda.'

Mrs. Villon regarded the youth composedly. 'It's all we have,' she said gently.

The bandit's voice was nearly a whisper. 'Lady, I'm trying to be nice about this. Get in the coach. I won't say it again.'

Kingdom, watchful and unspeaking, saw Mrs. Villon look first at Hollister, then at himself, and he read her thoughts: her husband was no coward, but physically incapable of preventing this; it must be to one of the other men that she look for help. She turned then, slowly, and walked to the stage. She stepped up, closed the door after her, and pulled the dust curtains.

Kingdom looked back to the robber to find the young man regarding him with idle interest.

'Haven't I seen you before?'

'No,' Kingdom said.

'Dallas, say? Maybe El Paso.'

'No.'

'Funny.' The bandit shook his head and looked at Villon, a merry grin touching his mouth. 'You should have put a few dollars in your wallet, friend. Would have thrown me off. Only an empty wallet on a prosperous-looking pilgrim—' He chuckled, gestured aimlessly with his gun and let the barrel slack to the pommel of his saddle. 'Just don't look right.'

Kingdom acted then, almost without thought, in the second that the man's attention was off him and his pistol unleveled. Kingdom was standing close to the head of the fellow's horse; he swung one great fist in a short upward arc that smashed with pile-driver painfulness into the skittish beast's nose.

The animal reared high with a sound of pain. The robber's response was unbelievably swift; as fast as thought itself, his gun was leveled and it crashed out at the very moment that the horse flinched from the blow. But that initial movement spoiled the shot, and he could not shoot again because he was fighting now to get his plunging horse under control.

Kingdom tried to catch the reins and missed. The man, cursing, fought his horse down; then turned the beast into Kingdom with a savage wrench just as Kingdom caught his reins and reached up to drag him from the saddle. The horse's shoulder hit Kingdom in the chest, tore away his hold and knocked him off his feet into the dust. The bandit's gun arced up again, and this time Kingdom was an easy and helpless target; then Hollister's whiplash shot out like the head of a striking adder—a living part of its wielder, as unerring as a third hand—and with a flat explosive crack, the bandit's gun was torn powerfully from his grasp and flung away.

Kingdom hauled himself dazedly to his hands and knees and saw his own gun lying where it had fallen only two yards away. He floundered toward it on his hands and knees, got it, and started to his feet, turning it on the bandit. With the same lightning celerity, the man clamped the reins with an iron hand, and spurred his horse straight at Kingdom and into him; Kingdom, only half upright, was again knocked sprawling.

Because he was unarmed now, the bandit did not stop but drove his horse on at a dead run into the desert. Kingdom was on his feet then, and shot after him twice; on the second shot, the horse collapsed beneath the man, throwing him far ahead.

Kingdom, unconsciously holding the gun pointed in front of him, started running without thinking toward the fallen horse, slowing with more caution as he neared it. He saw that the highwayman lay motionless beyond. The horse was kicking in death throes to which Kingdom put a stop with a third bullet.

Then with infinite caution he moved step by

step over to the bandit, wary of any trick. It was not until he actually stood over the man that the meaning of the grotesque angle at which his neck was twisted struck fully home to Kingdom. His hand, fisted around the gun butt, fell loosely to his side and he shivered and felt cold in this desert heat.

As he walked back to the coach, Mrs. Villon stepped from it and with the three men waited in silence as Kingdom stopped in front of them. He saw how her face showed the strain of the past moments, the skin stretched tautly white and nearly transparent over the delicate bones of her face.

She took a step toward him, her voice barely audible. 'We can't thank you. We can't begin to thank you.'

Kingdom looked at her dully, only half comprehending her words. Somewhere in the back of his mind a wordless voice was screaming that he should not have shot. The man had been riding away with his back turned; he should not have shot . . .

Hollister said in rough concern, 'What's wrong, son?'

'Nothing.' Kingdom drew the back of his hand across his eyes and looked at Hollister. 'You'll have to help me . . . He's dead. Neck's broken.'

CHAPTER FOUR

Lute lighted a huge black cigar and laid out a game of solitaire which he tried for five minutes to pretend he was enjoying, then threw down the card he was holding with an angry 'Ah-h-h—!' of disgust, relighted his dying cigar and leaned back in his chair.

Now, in the late afternoon, Ab's Keno Parlor in Boundary was nearly deserted, the only sound being the keno goose to the rear, and Lute had taken a front corner table to be alone and think. He was wondering in the gray fashion which had lately come to color his thoughts more frequently what the future could hold now. It seemed that with Doug's death the last possibility of escape from this life was ended. Too, Jim Kingdom would likely, blaming him for Doug's death, be on Lute's trail.

Lute's musing was broken by voices and by spurred feet clattering heavily on the walk outside, and two men in the nondescript denims of cowmen pushed through the batwings.

The first one came to a sudden stop in the center of the saloon, looking things over. He was over six feet, under thirty, his lower face yellow-blurred by a week's blond beard. His bone-white teeth clamped like a bulldog's on the cold cigar in his mouth.

The second man was an unshaven puncher with the look of the colorless drudge who spends all his life working for a bigger man's petty wages.

The tall man took the cigar from his mouth. 'Hey, Ab! You here?'

The owner raised his fat, balding head above the bar beneath which he was restacking glasses. He watched the two with no friendliness. 'We don't sell booze to you any more, Hassard. Not after the way you wrecked the place last time . . .'

'Yeah,' Hassard said. 'Bless you and keep you happy. Only I am good today regardless. Got a stage to meet . . . Alf and I just came in for a game while we're waiting.'

'I thought you were Santerre's segundo, not his errand boy,' Ab said with heavy sarcasm.

A kind of tidal flush worked up Hassard's neck. He said softly, 'Just take it easy.'

Ab snorted in disgust and turned his back on him.

Alf and Hassard sat down at a table by the wall; Alf produced a pack of age-slick cards from his jumper, and they played for a while, lackadaisically.

'This is peanuts,' Hassard said. 'Double the ante.'

'Then you drop me,' Alf said with a shake of his head.

'Hell,' Hassard said. He glanced over at

45

Lute. 'Want in, friend? Stud. Two-dollar ante.'

Lute hesitated; he had planned to go to bed early to get a full night's sleep and still be out of town early in the morning. But it was still pre-dark and he could stand to kill another hour or so. And he could use some money.

'I'll sit in for a couple hands,' he said.

Hassard dealt. He played with a hot-headed abandon which Lute judged might characterize his every action.

Hassard chewed the cigar. 'Raise you two?'

'Sure,' Lute said, but he watched their hands with a frown. Each had two cards, one face down. Lute's face-up card was an ace; Hassard's only a ten.

'Call you,' Lute said reluctantly.

Hassard grinned and slid a third card across the table to him. Lute's hand hid it briefly as he reached for it; then he turned it up—an ace. He looked mildly at Hassard who stared at the card, becoming very white. So, Lute thought, he knew what to expect.

Hassard said at last, thickly, 'I don't understand that ace.'

'I know,' Lute said. 'You expected this . . .' He threw a three seemingly out of nowhere to the table.

'You palmed it!'

'Yes.' Lute stood up, pocketing his silver. 'So I could find out what kind of a game I was in. Now I know, I'm out.'

Hassard smiled, almost idly. 'What're you

46

saying?'

'That you're a bellystripper,' Lute said quietly.

Hassard gently laid his cards on the table and leaned back in his chair. 'I'm waiting for you to say that again—only I don't think you will say it . . .'

Alf dropped his cards, his face turning faintly ashen under the dirt and whiskers. 'Egan, let it ride . . .'

'This whey-belly drifter worry you, Alf . . . Don't you let him. He won't say it. He won't say anything . . .'

Someone laughed over by the door and said, 'I think he will.'

Lute looked swiftly in that direction. The man who had spoken was so little concerned as to not even glance at them. He and a companion were both walking toward the bar now, the batwings swinging to behind them. They signaled for whiskey and bellied up to the bar without a glance at Hassard.

A kind of baffled anger mounted in Hassard's face. He said thickly, 'What did you say, Incham?'

Incham poured a drink, still not troubling to glance at Hassard, and said in a bored voice as though this were an old story to him, 'I said I think he will.'

'I'll argue that,' Hassard said thinly, something bright and hot kindling in his face.

Incham's companion threw his head back

and his long and clear-tinkling laughter lifted through the room, a mad and wild note of danger in it that made Lute's scalp prickle.

Hassard said sparely, 'How would you like to learn manners?'

The man stopped laughing; he leaned forward a little, barely lifting his voice above a whisper. 'You must make shift to give me a lesson, Mr. Hassard. Soon. Oh, very soon!'

'You are on the verge, Hassard,' Incham murmured, 'of making a very grave mistake. Tory is a little mad, you know . . .'

Hassard said thickly, 'This time we let it ride—'

'You're wise,' Incham said.

'Next time,' Hassard said. 'There'll be a next time.'

Tory clapped his hands. 'Encore . . . !'

'Be quiet, Tory,' Incham said irritably. He had turned back to the bar and was gazing absently at his drink, Hassard already forgotten.

Hassard pivoted on his heel and walked silently out, stiff with rage, Alf following.

Incham looked over his shoulder at Lute. 'Join us,' he said shortly.

Lute got up and walked over to the bar; Ab, behind it, said sourly to Lute, 'You damn fool,' and walked disgustedly to the rear of the room where he sat down with a two-months-old newspaper and ignored them. Tory threw his head back and laughed. Incham was sunk in brooding again and had apparently not even heard Ab.

Lute looked puzzledly at Ab, then at Tory. 'What was that for?'

'Ab doesn't approve of us,' Tory said merrily. 'He thinks you're taking up with bad company . . . Have a drink.'

Lute poured one, regarding the two men with unslackened interest. Their utter fearlessness in spite of their small stature was all that they held in common. Incham was in his forties, his thinning sun-bleached hair gray-streaked as he removed his hat. He seemed listless and bored, and Lute felt that this was a pose; there was a flicker of wicked arrogance behind the show-nothing opaqueness of the deep-set eyes. He wore a frayed and dusty suit, the coat open to show a threadbare linsey-woolsey shirt, and the trousers stuffed into jackboots. He carried no gun in sight. Far from being all-over impressive; but Lute sensed that wherever this man went, he would be the leader.

Tory was an effervescent opposite; the wickedness fairly danced through his dark eyes. He was about half Incham's age, the coal-black curls spilling from under his hat in startling contrast to his teeth which constantly showed in a laugh. There was a kind of Mephistophelian handsomeness to his face and about the sober black he wore from head to foot. The story of him could be read in an

49

instant in the tied-down Colt—butt pointed forward—at his left hip. It was somehow prominent, as through a part of the man; perhaps seeming so because it lay black against the unrelieved blackness of his clothes.

Tory had already had three quick drinks and was pouring himself a fourth. Incham looked at him suddenly, sharply. 'You've had enough.'

Tory paused in the act of lifting the glass and watched Incham with gleeful wickedness. 'Who says I have?'

Incham's pale eyes fixed him. 'I do.'

Tory set the glass down and gave another burst of mad laughter. He substituted a cigar for the drink and was still chuckling as he lighted it.

Incham ignored him and turned to Lute. 'I'm John Incham. This is Tory Stark.'

'Lute Danning,' Lute said and shook hands with both.

'I like your guts,' Incham observed. 'You're the first man I've seen who'd tell Hassard to his face that he cheated you. That's why I stepped in,' he added idly. 'You have too much nerve to die for it . . .'

Lute's throat tightened. 'I'm new here . . . I didn't know he was that good.'

Incham shrugged as though the subject held no real interest for him. 'He's good for a cowhand. Tory here could beat him. Knows it too.'

'That's obvious,' Tory said and laughed

50

some more.

Incham looked at him with irritation. 'I wonder if that brother of yours will ride in today? We've been waiting in town for two days now, and I'm sick of it.'

Tory shrugged. 'Maybe he's held up on business.'

'No doubt,' Incham said dryly, 'seeing that his business is holding up.'

Tory howled with laughter and banged his glass on the bar. Presently he sobered up enough to say, 'You'll be glad we waited for him, Mr. Incham. Bob, he wants much to join us. You wouldn't regret it if you waited another day. Or two days.'

'Or another week? Or two weeks?' Incham said sarcastically.

'He's hell on wheels with a gun,' Tory persisted.

'Better than you?'

Tory smiled enigmatically, thoughtfully. 'Like I told you, I don't know. He's three years younger than me, and we haven't seen each other much since the war ended. Got this letter from him awhile ago. First I heard of him in months . . . Maybe . . . we'll find out.'

Lute was beginning to understand now. This Incham was doubtless the head of a gang of wanted men; men from the backwash of the war years like Lute himself, cast up on the tidal beach of the raw frontier, a lawless frontier where they fell naturally into the

51

guerrilla and bushwhacker ways which had characterized their wartime tactics. Men like this Tory Stark. Perhaps like Lute Danning too.

At this idle thought, Lute felt a sudden and mounting excitement as the seed of an idea came to him. The excitement, at least, must have been apparent to Incham who smiled faintly and cocked a tawny eyebrow.

'You look as though you have a mouthful of hot meal, my friend, and your tongue scalding to get rid of it.'

Lute glanced at Ab, scowlingly absorbed in his newspaper, and lowered his voice. He talked quietly for ten minutes during which Incham said nothing, only giving him an occasional silent and appraising glance.

Finally, when Lute had ceased to speak and was watching the inscrutable Incham intently, expectantly, the man said thoughtfully, 'Your idea, now, Friend Lute—nothing new in the idea itself. Organized outlawry is an old story.'

'And it's paid off,' snapped Lute. 'It's the development of that organization ... Clockwork efficiency. Discipline. Military-type strategy and tactics ...'

'You need officers, trained officers, to whip 'em into shape,' Incham pointed out, and seeing the patient smile on his face, Lute felt withered. It was the same patient smile with which you would humor a child or an imbecile.

The gorge of anger rose in Lute; he drew a

52

deep breath. 'Look, Mr. Incham,' he said quietly. 'I know what I'm talking about. I only had a few years of schooling, but I always been a reader on field tactics. Books by military men. I ate the stuff. I used to read Caesar's Commentaries and Napoleon's Maxims over till the books fell apart.'

Incham's eyes sharpened on him. 'You mean it, don't you? You really think you've got something.'

'I damn well know I've got something.'

'All right, Napoleon. We'll see . . .'

'You mean—'

'You're welcome to come with us. Put your ideas to practical use if you like. I believe that every man should have ample apportunity to discover how much of a fool he can be.' Incham tempered his words with a faint smile. ' "We must hang together or assuredly we shall hang separately . . ." '

Tory laughed. 'That's a good one, Mr. Incham.'

'I didn't say it,' Incham said dryly, then lifted his head sharply. 'That's the stage horn. Would your brother be likely to come in on the stage?'

'He might stop it,' Tory chuckled, 'but not to get on it.'

'Doubtless,' Incham said. 'Still, we'll look.' He drained his glass, set it on the bar, and walked out, followed by Tory and Lute.

The westering sun softened in its last light

53

the harsh and raw outlines of the sprawling frontier outpost of Boundary as they stepped onto the walk. The arrival of the stage was always a thing to hold the attention; a small crowd was already gathering. The big Concord had just pulled up before Decatur's Mercantile across the street, the roiled dust of its stop already settling. The driver threw the lines around the brake, swung down from his high seat, and opened the door. A young woman and man were first down, followed by a nondescript little saddle bum.

Then the giant frame of the fourth passenger blocked the door, and a sudden half-recognized fear touched a cold finger to Lute's brain. Now the passenger had stepped down and the last rays of dying sunlight struck down on him fully there in the street.

Kingdom! He followed me here! Lute thought, and for a moment could not think beyond that; then he half-turned to take the step that would carry him back into the concealment of the saloon. It was too late. Kingdom's gaze had already swept up across the three men on the walk opposite; yet the glance must have been an absent one, for it moved on, idly, down the walk. Lute took a sidewise step then that put him in back of Incham, out of Kingdom's direct view.

Lute saw that the young woman had turned and spoken to Kingdom, who replied briefly, touched his hat, and walked past her to the boot to get his horses, leaving the young woman and her escort looking after him in surprise. Lute heard the woman's soft laughter.

The driver was talking, handing Kingdom his reins; Kingdom asked him something. The driver spoke and pointed downstreet and Kingdom started in that direction without a backward glance. Lute slowly, almost cautiously, let out his breath in relief and shivered in the fading light.

Tory said carelessly, 'He ain't on it,' and turned to walk back into the saloon, when Incham, staring intently at the stage, said curiously, 'Wait.'

Incham stepped off the walk and started across the street to the coach. Tory hesitated a moment, then followed him, Lute trailing after. They arrived at the stage with a few other onlookers, and Lute saw then what had attracted Incham's attention: the soles of a pair of boots on the floor of the stage, plainly visible through the open door. Beyond the boots, the blanket-covered figure told its own grim story.

'Dead man,' grunted Incham and reached through the door to draw the blanket away.

'A dead man,' Tory said disinterestedly. He shrugged. 'There's enough in the world.'

Lute caught the sharp, astonished jerk of Incham's shoulders as he bent through the doorway to examine the man, his body

55

blocking the others' view.

'Why,' he said in a soft, shocked voice which was, Lute considered, peculiar to his usual dispassionate tone.

The sound of it pulled even Tory to attention.

'Why, Tory,' Incham said, 'he looks enough like you to be—'

Perhaps he only then was struck with the significance of his own words. Incham looked at Tory, then back at the body; he reached out to draw the blanket too late.

Tory stood motionless for a moment, puzzling, his lazy poise slowly sloughing from him. Then Incham's words hit him with complete understanding, and his sudden movement forward was as swift as that of a striking snake. Incham barely stepped aside in time as Tory sprang up through the doorway. Lute heard Tory's single choked exclamation as he bent over the still figure.

Then Tory bolted through the doorway. In two strides he confronted the driver 'Which one . . . ?'

'Tory!' Incham said in a whiplash voice underscored with steel. Tory ignored him. The young couple, the saddle bum, and the driver looked at Tory in surprise.

'He kin of yours, son?' asked Hollister quietly.

'You can damn well see he is,' Tory breathed almost inaudibly, 'and if I have to blow the

56

guts from every one of you to get the—'

'Tory,' Incham repeated, altogether warningly . . .

Tory turned slowly. He said icily, dangerously, 'Mr. Incham—this is my business.'

'And mine,' Incham stated flatly. There was a long and tenuous pause . . . Incham's bleached eyes were no longer bored; they were suddenly agate-blue-bright, agate hard. 'And mine, Tory,' he repeated, his voice flattening into the monosyllabic tonelessness of an Indian's.

Tory's black gaze fixed Incham's blue one; it seemed that time hung still in eternity. Tory relaxed then, barely, without lowering his eyes.

'Why don't you ask,' Incham murmured, 'how your brother was killed rather than rant about like the mad idiot you are?'

'I don't care a damn how he was killed! One of these people done him in; that's all I care,' Tory said savagely. His eyes swept the driver and the passengers.

'Which one?' Tory said musingly. ' . . . You?' He looked the young woman's escort over, measuring his frail frame—then gave a cold laugh. 'No, not *you*!'

Tory's hot gaze raked on the saddle bum; the little man flinched instinctively; Tory's lip curled and he looked then to the driver who stood watching him with serene patience. 'There was another one,' Tory said.

'A big fellow . . . Where'd he go?'

Hollister said wearily, 'Picking daisies for all I know. Why don't you just take another look at the feller before you jump us any more, son? See how he died.'

Tory frowned at Hollister for a long time, then turned and walked, still frowning, back to the coachdoor and climbed in. After a moment he said in a puzzled way, 'He wasn't shot.'

'Looking for the wrong thing,' the driver said dourly. 'Neck's broke.'

Tory gingerly lifted the dead man's head, moved it, and lowered it gently. He said meagerly, 'How?'

'He held us up. He rode off fast; horse stumbled, threw him. That's how. His gear's back in the boot if you want it.'

'You sure none of you had a hand in it . . . ? You—that how it happened?' Tory looked at the frail young man.

The young man's jaw set. 'Yes,' he said coldly.

'Come off it, Tory,' snapped Incham. 'How else could it have happened?'

Tory didn't look at him. 'Where's his horse?'

Hollister looked Tory in the eye. 'Busted his leg when he stumbled. Shot him.'

'Ah,' Tory said softly. 'Two fatal breakages. It must have been *quite* a spill . . .'

'Are you through garnishing it?' Incham asked mildly.

Tory shot him a look of wrathful bafflement.

'I don't know,' he said, 'but—'

'Then quit it! I damn well know what you're trying to do. Your brother's dead and you're looking for someone you can take it out on. Face it. It was his own damn fault . . .'

Tory waited in a kind of hateful silence, and again looked to Hollister. 'I'm sorry,' Tory said with no apology in his tone. 'Will you do me the kindness of seeing that my brother is buried? And keep his gear.'

'Thanks, son,' Hollister said in a neutral voice. 'I'll do that.'

Incham, Tory and Lute left the group then and went without talk to the livery where they claimed their horses. Lute stopped at the hotel long enough to gather his scant belongings and check out. Rolling up his blankets, he congratulated himself on this windfall. He wouldn't need Doug after all, and Incham was an older and steadier head. Nor would he have to assemble men; the raw material was here.

As they rode out, passing the eating house, Lute glanced hungrily at it.

'We'll eat when we get to the home grounds,' Incham said. 'You'll like our little hamlet, Friend Lute. It's only ten miles' ride. After we eat, we'll talk plans—eh? I was halfway humoring you when I said we'd take you on, but the more I think about your military idea, the more I think you've got something.'

Ten miles on an empty stomach, Lute

59

thought morosely, and to take his mind off this depressing thought he asked: 'What kind of work you been doing till now?'

Incham smiled wryly. 'Mostly nothing. There's eleven of us in all. We're all wanted somewhere. Birds of a feather, you know . . . If there's a leader, I'm him by understanding. That's about all there is.'

Lute silently considered it a slovenly sounding outfit and was wondering if he could whip them into condition when Incham said with wry amusement, 'I know what you're thinking. But it's a lean country right now, Texas, even for an honest man, and no one has enough to be finicky about.'

Incham considered this briefly, then added, 'Me now. I just don't give a damn.' Incham shook his head. 'It's a hell of a way to be, Friend Lute. You think you know what you want—money, a ranch, what-have-you—then you get it and you know you don't want it . . .

'This idea of yours now,' he went on thoughtfully. 'It's not the money you mentioned. It's a fresh toy now—something new, you understand. In a week, a month, the novelty will wear off. Hell of a way for a Harvard graduate to be, isn't it?' And at the look of surprise on Lute's face, he nodded, and said, smiling, 'Oh yes.'

Tory, riding till now in dangerous silence, spoke. 'What are the men going to think about this?'

60

'Whatever I damn well tell them to think,' Incham said gently. He jogged along in the gathering darkness in muteness for a while, then said in sudden anger, 'Dammit, Tory, don't sound so cocky. I'm still top rooster on this dung-heap.'

Incham swiveled his head toward Lute, his bleached eyes faintly luminescent. 'You're the big brass, my boy, and it goes for you too. You're the general, but I'm commander in-chief ... Try to remember that. We'll all be happy ...'

Lute marked something about Incham then—that only his lips smiled, ever.

CHAPTER FIVE

Leaving the stage, Kingdom had been about to step to the boot to claim his horses when Mrs. Villon, at his side, spoke: 'There is no way we can begin to reward you for—you know.'

He shifted uncomfortably from one foot to the other and didn't reply.

She went on with a hesitant smile, 'Will we see you again?'

He looked at her, a little wonderingly. 'I don't know. Maybe.'

'But you will tell us your name, at least? You never did, you know ...'

A meager smile touched the lines of

Kingdom's face. 'Yes, ma'am. Davis,' he said. 'Jefferson Davis.' He touched his hat then, saw the surprise wash across her face and her husband's, and turned to walk to the boot where Hollister was unloading. He heard Mrs. Villon's quiet laugh behind him. Hollister looked up, grunted, and untied Kingdom's bay, handing Kingdom the reins.

'How much do I owe you?' Kingdom asked.

'This ride's on the line,' said Hollister, 'after the way you made a hero of yourself.'

'Thanks, only he would have gotten me without your using the whip.'

'Things work out,' Hollister grunted, passing the saddle to him.

'Which way to a place to sleep?'

'The Benton House's down the street. Next to last building on your right . . . So long, son.'

Kingdom turned his horses in at the livery, then registered at the hotel, paid for a night, and carried his gear up to his room. He stripped off his shirt and washed; then gloomily inspected in his palm the nine silver dollars remaining to him after breaking his last gold eagle . . .

Putting on another shirt from his warbag, not much cleaner than the one he'd had on, he sought the street. It was early dark now and the first lights showed in rectangular orange patches in the windows. He headed downstreet looking for an eating place he had seen on the way to the hotel. He saw it across the street and had stepped off the walk to angle across to it when he was hailed.

'You. Big fella. Hey!'

Kingdom stopped and squinted at the shadows under the mercantile gallery; a tall man stepped off the walk and came over to him, walking with a slight limp.

'Let's have the gun, brother,' he said, extending his hand.

Kingdom caught the glint of lamplight on the badge on his vest, but did not move. 'How come?'

'Town ordinance. No guns worn in the town limits. You check 'em at the jail from now on when you come in, pick 'em up when you leave.'

'Since when?'

'Since an hour ago,' the tall man said, satisfaction in his voice. 'I finally got the city council to vote on it. Been after them a month.' He snapped his fingers. 'Let's have it.'

Kingdom pulled Doug's Walker Colt from the waist of his trousers and passed it over. The tall man stuck it in his own belt and turned away with a nod. 'Get it from the jailer when you're ready to leave.' A light in the saloon across the street went on at that moment, a hazy illumination streaming out onto the street; it caught the tall man's profile as he turned.

'Pat Frost!' Kingdom said with a start.

The man turned to face him, a mild scowl

63

touching his fine aquiline features. 'I thought your voice was familiar, but where—'

'Spring of sixty-three—Leesville,' Kingdom said, watching him, a slow smile coming to his face. 'We were tent partners . . .'

Frost snapped his fingers. 'Jim Kingdom!' he rapped out, and grasped Kingdom's hand. 'Sure, I remember. Never did see each other after that . . . Leesville put me out of the war, Jim.'

'Didn't know but what you were dead, Pat. Looked for you after . . . among the dead and living.'

'Took a Minie ball through the leg. One of our own.' Frost chuckled and shook his head. 'Not so funny at the time, though. Spent the rest of the war in a half-dozen hospitals trying to save the damned thing.'

'So now you're sheriff or marshal here?'

'Marshal. Headed west after I was able to get around. Was sort of absorbed into this community. City council figured I'd make a town marshal of sorts . . . But you, Jim— what're you doing here? All you ever talked of was that family you were going home to. Something happen to them?'

'Nothing much . . . A long story, Pat. Tell it over a drink?'

'Never touch the stuff. How about over supper? Or you eaten?'

'No. Just going to.'

'Good! I was going home. Come on—Laura

can put on another plate . . . Staying here long?'

'No . . . You married? That's right—you used to tell me about your wife . . .'

He's got something, Kingdom thought, and a bleak and indefinable loneliness settled in his mind.

They hauled up on a side street then, and Pat led the way up a sycamore-shaded pebbled path to a small lighted house. They tramped up on the porch, walking in through the propped-open door. The front room was small, the furnishings bright and comfortable.

Pat sailed his hat into a chair. 'Laura!'

'In the kitchen, Pat.'

'Come out here a minute . . . An old friend of mine came in today. Want you to meet him.'

She came out of the kitchen, a tall, red-haired young woman whose slim face, flushed from stove heat, was pleasant when she smiled. 'Laura, this is Jim Kingdom. We were tent partners during the war.'

Kingdom took off his hat, nodding self-consciously.

'Hello,' she said and smiled. 'Pat used to tell me about you . . . You'll stay for supper, Mr. Kingdom? It's all ready.'

'I already invited him . . . Come on in the kitchen, Jim.'

Kingdom had three helpings of beef stew, the first decent meal he'd had in months, and though he was never particular he appreciated

65

the difference. He quietly envied Pat. The marshal said nothing until Kingdom had leaned back in his chair with a cigarette while Laura cleared the table.

'Anything particular bring you here, Jim?' Frost prodded gently.

This was business to Frost as much as friendly curiosity, Kingdom knew. He explained in a few words.

'Mm,' Pat said thoughtfully. 'Melanie Hassard, eh? I know the girl you mean . . . She married some wild young fellow—a drifter. Damn! I remember. His name was Kingdom too—but I never thought to connect . . . Well, she runs the rooming house. That's across the street from my jail . . .'

Kingdom stirred in his chair. 'I'd best be getting to see her.' He stood. 'Thank you for the meal, ma'am. Very good.'

He walked to the front door, Frost following him, pipe in hand. At the door, Kingdom put on his hat and turned to shake hands with Pat.

'Good luck, Jim. Hope you don't come across this fellow Lute you're looking for in my town. Hate to run *you* in for something like that.'

'I'm not looking for him,' Kingdom said, 'but if I find him, I think I'm going to hurt him.'

Pat grinned. 'Right. Come and see me before you leave.'

Kingdom said he would, and they parted.

Kingdom paused outside the rooming house. It was two stories, the warm light of the windows a comfortable and homelike thing. He stepped up on the porch and knocked. The door opened almost immediately. A young girl of about nineteen in a beige-gray dress stood there. The look on her face was wondering as she regarded him, and this altered suddenly into a wild happiness and she took a step toward him and the happiness faded and some of the life went out of her eyes. But the wonderment remained. She stepped back, holding the door open.

'I thought you were someone else. Please come in.'

He stepped inside, pulling off his hat and looking around, then settling his gaze again to the girl before him. 'Mrs.—Kingdom?'

'Yes.' She was not tall, was very dark, and had a strong, earthy, almost coarse prettiness that held no appeal to him though he judged that Doug would find it most attractive.

'I'm Doug's brother,' Kingdom said. The puzzlement left her face; a kind of welcoming warmth came to it.

'Jim,' she smiled. 'Of course. He spoke of you so much, I always thought I'd know you right away. You do look alike . . .'

She led the way into an adjoining room. There was a long dining table reaching the length of the room; it was still uncleared as though the roomers had finished eating shortly before. Melanie pulled out two chairs and sat down, smoothing her skirt.

'I'm sorry Doug isn't here, Jim ... He's been gone for several weeks. But he must have written you about us ... Of course, or you wouldn't be here.'

Kingdom mumbled something and looked at his hat again.

'I haven't really seen much of Doug since we were married. That was six months ago.' A shade crossed her face ... 'He has to get out sometimes—to travel and such. But he'll tire of that. He ...' The defiance crumpled suddenly and evaporated into misery; she said in a low, passionate voice, 'I keep telling everyone that, Jim ... I don't care what they think, but I keep telling myself the same. It's no use to pretend to you—you know what he is ...' She bit her lip, tears starting from her eyes.

He played for time, time in which to gauge the saying of this. 'How did—how did you happen to meet?'

She wiped her eyes. 'I used to bring food to the prisoners at the jail. They had put him there over night—for getting drunk, he said. We wanted to get married almost right away, but—I have a brother too ... And what a brother he is.' Her voice was soft and bitter-edged. 'Since Pap and Mam died, he has delegated himself to tell me how to live—what men I can associate with, how to run my business . . .'

'Your brother didn't want you to marry Doug? In his place, can't say I'd blame him . . .'

'You don't understand. You couldn't—not unless you know Egan. He likes to ride rough-shod. Anything that he owns, or feels he owns, he has to break and crush. What anyone else believes or cares is nothing to him if it conflicts with what he wants. I used to do as Egan told me because it was easier to give in than to always fight him. Then he married a girl he couldn't control, and—well—I guess her example helped me to fight back. Poor Egan. Between the two of us, we nearly drove him crazy.'

Melanie hesitated. 'It didn't do him any good. He's . . . He's changed into something I can't name. He drinks and gambles away his wages and picks a fight on the least excuse. That's why his condemning Doug is so stupid . . .'

Filled with a deep pity for the girl, Kingdom said gently, 'But you and Doug were married after all . . . Your brother bother you since?'

'He sees me about twice a week. Always to tell me that one of the times Doug rides off, he won't come back. Egan says I likely won't see him again this time. Sometimes,' she burst out suddenly, 'I think he's right!'

'This time,' Kingdom said carefully, holding back no longer, 'he is.'

69

Her eyes lifted; a fear widened in them. 'Jim—what do you know . . . ?'

'Doug's dead,' Kingdom said with a flat and nearly intentional brutality which he could not help because these things were utterly strange to him. 'What I came here to tell you, ma'am. I've been looking for him two years. Finally caught him a couple days ago in a little town northeast of here—Dry Springs—'

'You—' she whispered. 'You—'

'No!—I didn't.' He looked bitterly at his hat brim. 'I don't know what I would have done. But I didn't have time to do anything. He was shot by a trigger-happy kid . . .'

Kingdom did not look at her after that, but he could not close his ears to her soft choking sobs. Vaguely, he was aware of the back door opening quietly, and he glanced up, seeing through the open doorway between kitchen and dining room that a man had stepped into the kitchen and was looking around. It was Loomis, the little bum from the stage. He must be boarding here, Kingdom thought absently, and, having missed the supper hour at some saloon, was entering by way of the kitchen in the hope of wheedling something to eat . . .

Kingdom stood up, knowing that he must leave this girl in her grief; there was nothing, nothing at all, he could do for her. He turned wordlessly toward the front room, and had not taken two steps when Loomis' voice, strung like the twang of a tightened wire, came from the doorway to the kitchen.

'Turn around, you, and don't move.'

Kingdom looked over his shoulder; Loomis had pulled his gun and was trying to hold it on both of them, the barrel wavering from side to side in a ragged circle.

Loomis licked his lips. 'I want all the money you got, lady. Get it.'

Melanie slowly lifted her eyes and looked at the little man dully. She got to her feet with a tired and dragging movement. She faced Loomis directly—then began to laugh. She laughed with a wild unrestraint which mounted to a shrill note of hysteria. A primitive chill ran up Kingdom's spine at the sound.

Loomis stared at her; his jaw dropped. A gleam of fright touched his faded eyes. He had not anticipated behavior like this. His voice was panicked. 'Stop it, lady! I'm telling you stop it!'

Melanie threw her head back; she laughed all the more shrilly; with a birdlike movement, she stepped suddenly to a highboy against the wall, opened it, and came out with a heavy pistol, which she swung to train on Loomis.

Loomis hesitated as any man will when it is a woman who threatens him, and his hesitation nearly cost him his life. As it was, the two guns crashed as one shot. The girl could not handle the heavy weapon's recoil; it bucked and the slug whined far to Loomis' right. Then she was driven into the highboy, bent half across it, and

71

fell from there to the floor.

In one unbelievable moment of violence it was finished; too swiftly for Kingdom's slow and methodical mind to fully grasp, the girl's still form was lying at his feet, and he regarded it briefly in a kind of obscure horror. Then he looked at Loomis who stared at the girl, paralyzed into momentary immobility by the shocking enormity of what he had done.

Then Loomis, his gun falling loose in his hand, retreated backward to the door, making a whimpering sound in his throat. Kingdom came to his senses at the same moment and a white-hot wrath lifted in him, and he lunged after Loomis. Melanie's gun had fallen by Kingdom's feet and he did not even think of it, wanting only to get his great bare hands on this man. He reached the doorway and lunged through it without a pause, straight at Loomis.

Kingdom saw the panic in Loomis' face and then Loomis' pistol barrel swinging at his eyes in a wild, vicious arc; and Kingdom saw no more except mushrooming lights around a penumbra of blinding pain. The blow drove him to his hands and knees, and, sickened with the pain, he had to fight to retain consciousness. Catching the edge of a table in one hand, Kingdom hauled himself doggedly to his feet. The back door was open.

Loomis was gone.

Kingdom staggered to the door and leaned against the doorjamb for support. He could see only a dipping vale of prairie in the empty darkness out there; Loomis was swallowed by the night. Kingdom moved back into the room, putting his hand to his head. Where the edge of Loomis' gun muzzle had caught him, on the dirge of his forehead just over his nose, he was bleeding a little, not much. He wiped at it mechanically with his sleeve and walked slowly back to the dining room where the girl lay crumpled in a little motionless heap on the floor. Without thinking, he bent down and picked up the gun she had dropped. He looked down at her; her face, mercifully, was turned away.

He walked a few aimless steps away, to let the sick rage ebb from him, the gun still unconsciously grasped loosely in his hand, and became aware of voices outside.

Kingdom walked to the front door and was reaching to open it when it was flung open in his face. A tall, yellow-haired man charged through the doorway into him, almost knocking both of them down.

The man swore and stepped back, staring at Kingdom, 'Well, who the hell—'

Pat Frost was in back of the fellow and pushed roughly past him. 'What's happened, Jim? What—'

Kingdom nodded toward the dining room.

The yellow-haired man shoved Kingdom aside and pushed ahead of Pat into the dining room. Kingdom walked slowly after them.

Before he reached the dining-room entrance, he heard the yellow-haired man's voice, soft with a note of pure horror.

'Melanie ...!' A pause. 'My God. She's—she—'

Kingdom heard Frost rap out sharply then, 'Egan!'

The man was standing to face Kingdom suddenly as he reached the doorway. There was a sustained sheen of madness in his eyes that brought Kingdom to a dead halt. The man had opened his mouth to speak when his gaze fell on the gun still in Kingdom's hand.

'My God!' he breathed. 'He used her own gun ...'

His hand whipped back his coat, closing with incredible swiftness on a holstered pistol there. Frost, anticipating this, had already moved to his side, his gun out. As the man drew, the barrel of Pat's weapon descended in a swift short arc across his skull. He pitched forward on his hands and knees. Pat picked up the gun and shoved it into his belt.

'I'd about talked him into handing it over when we heard that shot,' Pat remarked. 'Probably would have had to do this to get it regardless. Anyway, it was the only way I could stop him just now short of shooting him ...'

'This the brother?'

'That,' Pat said dryly, 'is the brother. A prize package, is he not?' His jaw set a little then, as though in shame of his unthinking levity in the face of what had happened.

Hassard was trying to push himself up, moving his head slowly, feebly, to and fro. Pat holstered his gun, bent down and caught him roughly under the arms, hoisting him to his feet and letting go of him. Unsupported on his feet, Hassard staggered off balance, caught at the wall, and leaned there. His eyes focused on Kingdom with a concentrated hard brilliance.

Hassard looked at Pat then and said bitterly, 'He must be a friend of yours, Frost.'

'He's my friend,' Pat said flatly, 'which is why I don't have to ask—I know he didn't kill your sister.'

'You seem to have decided that already!'

'And you've already settled in your head he's guilty. What's that—the gospel according to Hassard?' Frost looked at Kingdom. 'Let me see the gun, Jim?' He took it and broke it. 'One bullet gone, all right.'

Hassard snatched the gun from him and sniffed it. 'Fresh fired, too.' He lifted his hot gaze to Pat. 'How much more you need, Frost?'

'She shot,' Kingdom said evenly, 'at the man who killed her.'

'Then how come there was only one shot?'

'Be quiet, Egan,' Pat said irritably. 'How did it happen, Jim?'

Kingdom told him.

Hassard said with a deep long-ingrained bitterness, 'So both guns went off at once. And

75

the little man vanishes into the night. It's too pretty, dammit, Frost. Can't you see ... Wait a minute.' He looked for a long moment at Kingdom. 'What happened to the bullet Melanie fired—if she fired it?'

'Where would it have gone, Jim?' Pat asked.

'In the kitchen, from the way they were standing, I judge ...'

Hassard and Frost inspected the kitchen to locate the slug; Pat leisurely, Hassard with a fevered intensity. They found nothing. Hassard glanced at Kingdom, an acid comment ready, when Pat asked suddenly, 'Did you open the back door, Jim?'

'No. The tramp left it open.' Kingdom added dryly, 'He left in a hurry.'

'There's your answer, Egan.'

'Answer to what?' Hassard snapped.

'The door to the dining room here and the back door are in line with where your sister was standing, over there by the highboy,' Frost said patiently. 'If the killer was standing in the doorway to the dining room like Jim said, and the bullet Melanie fired missed, it likely went on through the back doorway.'

'It likely did,' Hassard said with heavy irony. 'Should we take a lantern and go out and look for the bullet? God, what a joke your law is!'

'That nick on Jim's head is no joke,' Pat said, his patience on a fast down-wane.

'She probably gave it to him fighting him off,' Hassard said, his frustrated rage carrying him beyond caution.

Kingdom shifted a little on his feet, his deep-set eyes burning on Hassard. Pat said dryly, 'You ought to be nicer to him, Egan ... You're practically related.' Hassard stared at him. 'Doug Kingdom's brother.'

'*His* brother ...? Yes, he looks like him.' Hassard spat the words as though they were an anathema. 'So he thought he'd take over where brother left off.'

'That's just about all out of you, Egan!'

'Is it? What about now—he goes free, eh?'

'He stays at my house tonight,' Pat said caustically. 'We'll hold the inquest tomorrow. Suit you?'

'You better lock your doors and windows tonight,' Hassard mocked. He turned his back on them and walked slowly back to where his sister's body lay. They left him then, Kingdom preceding Pat out the door. They started side by side across the street.

'I'll drop these guns off at the jail, then we'll get some sleep,' Pat said wearily. 'I don't have to tell you how sorry I am about this, Jim.' He sighed. 'I hope it doesn't upset any plans you have.'

'No,' Kingdom said absently, his mind weighted with all that had happened.

Melanie had wanted to die, Kingdom was sure. But Hassard, with his vibrant and violent passions, would never see that. Nor would Hassard, carried by his own convictions, ever

77

be convinced that another than Doug's brother had shot his sister. Looking ahead, Kingdom could see only trouble.

CHAPTER SIX

For Hassard, there was no warmth in the afternoon sun as he stood with his back against the tie-rail in front of his sister's rooming house, chewing on a dead cigar. He only stood, favoring the hurt of Melanie's death as a dog favors a bad leg. He scarcely looked up when fifteen-year-old Murray Ambergard, his youngest rider, walked up to him with the angular grace of early adolescence.

Hassard took the cigar from his mouth, frowning. 'Why ain't you at the ranch?'

'Boss sent me in, Egan. To find out why you didn't bring his daughter and her husband in yesterday . . .'

'The stage was late,' Hassard growled, his gaze shifting to the marshal's office. 'I carried their stuff over to the hotel last night. They stayed there . . . Damn it all, kid—you know's well as anyone how Hollister keeps a schedule. So does Frenchy.'

'I know,' Murray said. 'I already talked to Mrs. Villon over at the cafe. She says for you to drive the wagon over to the hotel and pick up their luggage so's they can go out to the

78

ranch right away.'

'Does she?' Hassard said disinterestedly, still moodily watching the jail. He wondered with a sudden anger if Kingdom had slept well last night. A warm bed instead of a cold cell for Melanie's killer, he thought. And this morning, at the inquest, the coroner's jury had favored Kingdom's story, absolving him of blame. The cigar was tasteless; Hassard spat it savagely into the street.

Murray shifted from foot to foot, waiting, and when Hassard didn't speak, he said uncomfortably, 'What should I tell her, Egan?'

Hassard looked at him with the stir of a vast irritation which heightened as he recalled Ab's words of yesterday afternoon: I thought you was Santerre's segundo, not his errand boy . . . 'Why,' he said, turning the words with slow relish on his tongue, 'you run tell Mrs. Villon to go to hell.'

Murray's jaw fell; he became stilled in his tracks as though rooted to the ground, staring at Hassard.

'Go on!' Hassard roared. 'Tell her!'

Murray backed away, his mouth open; then turned and broke into a trot, headed for the café. Hassard took out a fresh cigar. Well, that does it. I'm through at the ranch, he thought; and at the moment he didn't care a damn.

He pushed away from the tie-rail and was cutting across the street toward Ab's when Mrs. Villon stepped out of the China Café and headed down the walk to meet him. Oh Lord, here it comes, Hassard thought tiredly. She stepped off the walk and came up to him in the middle of the street.

'Mr Ambergard delivered your message, Mr. Hassard,' she said very quietly. 'I only wanted to tell you that if you have any business here that is that important, we will be glad to wait . . . I'm sorry—of course it's your sister . . . You'll want to stay for her funeral.'

'My sister, yes.' Hassard stirred impatiently, wanting to get on to Ab's.

'I'm sorry the man wasn't caught, sir.'

'Begging your pardon, ma'am,' Hassard said bitingly, 'they had him, then let him go.'

'Do you mean—Mr. Kingdom? Oh, no. I heard of that, but you're mistaken . . . At the risk of his own life, he saved my husband and me from being robbed yesterday.'

'Shot the robber too. Heard about that . . . Two killings in one day . . .'

'Really, Mr. Hassard—you can't truly believe that he killed your sister? I am certain that Mr. Kingdom—'

In a sudden furious irritation, Hassard broke in, 'You seem almighty concerned about *Mister* Kingdom, lady . . . Maybe your husband would enjoy hearing just how concerned. Go on,' Hassard taunted, a final shred of discretion falling from him. 'Go tell that big bad husband of yours how the nasty man insulted you so he can come and whip me out

80

of town.'

'Yes,' she said in a low voice, 'and he would try.' Her chin lifted. 'You don't like women, Mr. Hassard.' She did not question, merely affirmed.

'Not any.'

'Yet you had a sister, and you must have had a mother.'

Hassard said in a hard voice, 'Drinking runs in our family ... She was never sober long enough to be a mother. Look, lady—if I'm fired, say so.'

'Fired? For what?'

' ... Saying things.'

She laughed almost silently. 'Fire you? What good would that do?'

'I know,' grunted Hassard. 'You'll wait till we're back at your old man's ranch, then tell him, and have the pleasure of watching me whipped off the place—or shot.'

Her expression altered into one of open, scathing contempt. 'No one will hear of it.'

He frowned, watching her with wary suspicion. 'Why?'

'Why?' she repeated, musingly. 'Well, sir, insulting a woman seems to make you most proud. Now who would I be to spoil a beautiful ideal like that?' She turned away, walking back toward the café, her small back very straight. Hassard, watching her go, felt a deep shame, but it was only momentary.

He pivoted on his heel and walked on to

81

Ab's. An hour later in the hot and muggy afternoon, he was still there, thoroughly drunk—not fuzzy-unsteady drunk; cold-ice drunk, the fury in him building and piling, tier on tier. The man who had killed his sister was free . . .

With a quiet intensity he surveyed the scattering of loafers. His gaze settled finally on a small group playing stud at a corner table. One of the men was George Taine, a short wicked-tempered man in the disreputable dignity of a whiskey-soiled suit and neither washed nor shaven as usual. He'd had a good freighting business which he had mostly drunk and gambled away. But the fool still commanded an aura of respect, Hassard considered; at least among the crowd at Ab's who were his kind.

This was his man, Hassard knew.

Carrying his glass, Egan walked over to Taine's table, saying. 'How are you, George,' as he clapped Taine on the shoulder with one hand and reached for Taine's bottle with the other. ' . . . George, you ought to get an apron and be your own bartender.'

Taine brought his fist down with a crash on the bar just between Hassard's hand and the bottle. Hassard swore and jerked his hand back, though he was expecting this.

'Just keep your damn hands off my bottle,' Taine said, working the words out slowly and thickly. 'Nobody touchin' my bottle . . .'

'That's right,' Hassard said softly, 'that's right, George. Sorry.' Taine was in the state he had counted on.

'Another thing. I never wore no apron, damn you. You go round telling no one I wore no apron.'

'I never said you wore no apron,' Hassard began patiently, then broke off, looking intently into Taine's face. 'Why, hell, fella—you need a drink.' He sloshed Taine's glass full from Taine's bottle and poured one for himself. 'On me, kid,' Hassard said generously.

'Thank you,' Taine said with dignity; they drank in companionable silence for several moments. The other men grinned to themselves.

'Heard about your sis, Egan,' Taine mumbled. 'That's a pow'ful sorry thing. Really is.'

'Thanks, George,' Hassard said somberly. An hour before, he would have hit Taine for mentioning his dead sister's name in a saloon; now it was only a prime excuse for the unfolding of his idea. Hassard smiled with drunken thoughtfulness and gave Taine a sidelong glance. 'Hear how she died, George . . . ?'

Taine said he hadn't. Hassard told him his own version of the story. Several others became interested and listened.

'Fella who shot your sis is still running loose?' Taine asked with inebriate gravity, and when Hassard nodded, George clucked sympathetically and shook his head.

'If that ain't a pack of hell,' said Taine. 'What the hell is there a state of affairs like that for?'

'The law says he didn't do it,' Hassard said sadly. 'Man has to go with the law, George . . . The law says so.' He watched Taine slyly.

'Law, hell!' said a tough. 'What good's your damn law for this . . . ?'

Hassard struck while the iron was hot. He said: 'She had a big heart, Mellie did . . . Many's the time she let some drunk sleep in her place when the jail was full up—you boys among others I recall.'

'That's so, yeah,' a loafer said.

'So she did,' Ab said casually over by the bar, swabbing it with a colorlessly dirty rag, 'until Egan made her quit.'

'Yes, I made her quit,' Hassard snapped. 'Wasn't fitting a woman should be inviting men into her house to sleep off liquor, boarding house or not.'

'Ain't fitting you should be talking about a lady, a dead lady too, in a saloon, your sister too,' Ab said gently. It was a kindly hint that the discussion end here.

Hassard shrugged; he had only wanted to make these men recall the goodness of Melanie, to rankle a bit over the injustice of her killer going free. His part was done; from here on, he could depend on George Taine to

84

take the bit in his teeth, and George was all the spur that they needed . . .

Hassard bought everyone a drink.

'A damn fine girl,' someone muttered.

Hassard bought everyone another drink.

Taine swung suddenly to Hassard, frowning and at least half sobered. 'Damn it, Egan. We all liked Melanie . . .'

'So did I, George,' Hassard said, lifting a shoulder. 'Only what can we do? Besides, he's innocent. Half a dozen public-spirited citizens said so this morning at the inquest . . .'

Taine said with great gentleness, 'Just show him to us.'

'We're with you, George,' a man shouted; a swift clamor broke out.

'Name the play, Egan,' growled Taine.

'Get a rope,' Hassard said, grinning. 'I'll name it . . .'

CHAPTER SEVEN

'It's a shame, Pat, that's all,' his wife said with controlled indignation, cleaning up the supper dishes with a louder clatter than usual. 'I really don't see why Jim should leave so soon.'

Pat took his pipe from his mouth, lifted a shoulder in a spare shrug and dropped it. 'You can't talk to Egan Hassard, my dear. The coroner jury's verdict was a fraud to him. He will want Jim's head.' His pipe had gone out and he irritably knocked it empty on the edge of his thick china coffee cup, then picked up the cup and moodily swirled the dregs aimlessly about, watching the ashes dissolve murkily into them.

Finally Pat set the cup on the table and glanced up at Kingdom. 'You'll have to get out of town, Jim.'

Kingdom pushed his empty plate back and stood up. 'I'll make it early tonight.'

'You will, like hell! Sit down. I'm not chasing anyone out at night.'

Kingdom shook his head. 'It has to be tonight, Pat. Hassard won't stop here. He'll burn your house down to get me. You've had enough trouble on my account. It'll stay light long enough for me to put enough distance between me and Boundary to make it worth while.'

'Forget it, Jim. Hassard won't strike tonight.'

As though in reply, a rock crashed through the single high little kitchen window and fell to the floor in a shower of jangling glass. Frost lunged for the door and swung it open; whoever had flung the rock was gone. Frost turned slowly back into the kitchen.

Kingdom watched him narrowly, saying quietly, 'You see, Pat? It's started already. Hassard or another. It has to be now.'

Before Frost could reply, there was a loud

knocking at the back door. Frost opened it a cautious inch or so, then threw it wide; lanky Bud Casement, Frost's night deputy, came in, his long face rock-set.

'Hassard, Pat. He's been talking it up in Ab's. He's got that bunch of saloon bums primed for a lynching. We can't stop it. They're set to string us up too if we try. Only thing to do is get him,' he jerked his head toward Kingdom, 'out of town.'

Pat looked wryly at Kingdom. 'Now you're in it, kid.'

'So are you,' Kingdom said grimly. 'How can I get my horse? I can't show my face out there.'

'A detail, James,' Pat said. 'You pack up your gear quickly, I'll go to the office to fetch your gun, and Bud here will go to the livery to saddle your horse. We'll both meet him there. Okay, let's go . . .'

Pat was standing, as planned, in the archway of the livery, beckoning frantically to Kingdom, who lunged onto the walk and broke into a run for the archway, burdened with the gear. He had covered half the distance when there was a shout from the hotel and the crash of a pistol, and the ground between his running legs was ruptured violently, spraying his boots with exploding clods of dirt.

Kingdom reached the archway and ran on down the runway to the rear of the store where Casement was holding his bay. Kingdom threw the saddle on and cinched it swiftly; he'd have to leave the packhorse ... He heard the crash of Pat's rifle. Kingdom swung into the saddle as Pat came running back from the archway, telling Bud to take his place. Casement hurried to the front of the livery. From his belt, Frost pulled Kingdom's gun and passed it up to him, then grasped his hand.

'You'll have to ride out the back, Jim. They know you'll be leaving that way; they'll try to circle and cut you off.' He paused, still holding Kingdom's hand. 'My jurisdiction ends where the town ends. Out there, Hassard can get you without breaking any law. You'll be free game in an open field ... So hyper like hell and good luck.'

Kingdom raised a hand in parting salute and spurred the bay lightly; he responded to the touch, heading out the rear gate. There was another shot from the front. Kingdom put the horse onto the plain, heading to the west.

He went at an easy clip for a mile, not looking back, and when he finally topped a rise to pause and scan his back trail, he felt no surprise to see the dust shroud of pursuers just leaving town. They know his line of flight, then.

Kingdom turned at almost right angles to his original direction, hoping to send them on a false beeline into the desert. This hope dissolved into futility; the land was too open, too rolling. He had not gone a half-mile before he could see that the horsemen had turned off his original route and were cutting at an easy angle toward his new direction. He had done nothing except decrease his margin of safety; his maneuver had only lessened the distance between his pursuers and himself. His only chance now, Kingdom knew, was to outrun them or outlast them.

He set the bay into a mile-eating pace onto a straightaway course of hard-packed grassland rolling miles ahead. The bay was a stayer, just getting his first wind. Kingdom held him in.

The miles blurred past, the character of the land unchanging. Then the grass grew patchy and the face of the ground became raw and barren. Before Kingdom knew it, he was heading into brush. He cut quickly off and away from it. These men were familiar with this land; it wouldn't do to play hide-and-seek with them in brush country. But the move again severely narrowed the distance between him and those behind. He did not hold in now, but let the bay have his stride. Too late . . .

Kingdom heard the shots then and felt the horse's pace break. Hit, he thought, with a sinking in him. For all that he could do, the horse was slowing, the rhythmic beat of hoofs slackening, faltering beneath him . . .

They thundered on. The time came when the riders were so near he could hear their shouts. Kingdom felt the ground dip beneath him and he raced down a gentle slope into a thinly timbered vale where the skyline cut him off from view of them.

The opposite side of the vale sloped up more steeply and at its crest was a dense wall of chaparral. Kingdom decided to find cover there, even if he had to leave the horse. It couldn't take him much farther regardless. He put it up the steep gradient of the slope now and was halfway to the top when the townsmen came into view, riding down into the dip. He was a plain target now, and on the first shot the bay reared back, mortally hit this time. Kingdom kicked free of the stirrups and jumped clear of the falling animal as its weight sloughed sideways.

Kingdom floundered on his hands and knees in the soft earth, then was on his feet, his boots digging hard at the loose dirt as he plunged on up the slope toward the chaparral. The chaparral was only three yards away . . .

Then a rifle rashed out from the chaparral, almost in his face it seemed. The flash of it in the growing dusk washed into Kingdom's eyes and blotted out his sight for a moment. He stopped in his tracks, his first thought one of crushing panic, that part of his pursuers had somehow maneuvered in front of him and had ambushed him. Then Kingdom heard the owner of the rifle, crouched up there out of his view, call harshly:

'Come on, you damn fool!'

Kingdom began his running climb again, and as he went past two stunted Judas trees at the summit, found himself at the fringe of the chaparral. He dived unheedingly into it, landing with a wind-driving grunt on his side. He found himself sprawled beside the rifleman who shot again, and Kingdom heard the scream of a horse. He squirmed around on his belly to face into the vale and saw that the pursuit had reached the bottom of the slope on this side, that one of their horses was down kicking and that they had stopped, milling disconcertedly.

The rifleman shot again.

They turned their horses; one rider gave the unhorsed man a hand up behind him, and the entire body of nearly a dozen men turned and retreated. One rider alone hesitated, looking up toward the chaparral, his horse fiddle-footing beneath him; then he turned it, riding after the others. In the failing light, Kingdom could not have seen the man's face from this distance, but he knew that it was Hassard.

The rifleman eased himself slowly to his feet, looking after the riders. Kingdom stood up and watched too for a moment, then thrust his gun back into the waist of his trousers and looked at the man beside him. Kingdom felt a vague surprise at the grating sound of his own voice:

'I ought to thank you.'

The man turned to regard him measuringly.

'Not when you do it that way.' He seemed to look at Kingdom more closely then, and Kingdom knew that his face, even in the growing darkness, must have showed the harried strain of these last days, for the man's tone was more kindly. 'They laying a bounty for you, son?'

Kingdom felt a vast and weary irritation sweep him. 'Ask my horse.'

'Well, now, hard on a man.'

'And on a horse. What place is this?'

The man's frosty gray eyes regarded him sharply. He was of about middle age, Kingdom judged; tall and gaunted, burned Indian-dark by years of desert wind and sun, his face weather-tracked like seamed mahogany. An untrimmed roan mustache hid half his mouth.

'You don't know?' he said slowly, and when Kingdom shook his head the man let his rifle, which he had been holding half leveled on Kingdom, slacken a little in his hands. 'You didn't know this was Incham's valley?'

'Was I supposed to?'

'I figured so, seeing you came in with a posse salting your tail.' The gaunt man waited a moment and when Kingdom did not speak, he said, 'My name's Teal.'

Kingdom nodded and said nothing.

Teal laughed. 'Maybe you're right,' he said. 'Come on. You can talk to Incham then.'

'Who's Incham?'

Teal had half turned away; now he looked

back at Kingdom intently. 'You never heard of Incham?'

Kingdom shook his head in negation.

'Well, this should be interesting,' Teal said dryly.

CHAPTER EIGHT

Kingdom stripped saddle and bridle off his dead horse and walked back up to where Teal waited.

'Watch out for the brush,' Teal said, and started down a trail broken erratically through the chaparral. He must have followed it by instinct, for it was invisible in this light, and so nonexistent in some places that he had to force a way with his rifle barrel. Kingdom fought his way after Teal, stumbling, grunting, sweating, scratched and beaten by lashing, backswinging branches.

The chaparral ended suddenly, the trail breaking onto an open bank clustered with ocotillo clumps and grease-wood. It dipped away and down steeply up here, sloping off gradually at the bottom and spreading away into a small, surprisingly heavily timbered valley. From here, one caught a panoramic view of the land: timbered with scrub oak and elm, hackberry, and where he caught a glint of water somewhere below, cottonwoods and perhaps willows. The water explained the verdancy, rare enough in this part of Texas to make Kingdom simply stand and look.

The valley itself was bowl-shaped, surrounded by the great ringlike dune on which they stood. The broad flat crest of the dune was, as far as he could tell, fringed all around by the thick and nearly impenetrable jungle of chaparral, as perfect a natural barrier as he had ever seen.

Teal let him look his fill, then remarked, 'It got me the same way. Let's move.'

Kingdom followed him gingerly, sliding and stumbling, down the steep bank. It was not until they were on the gently off-leveling lower slope that Kingdom saw the buildings thrown up here and there among the trees. As they started along a footpath leading into the trees, he saw that the dwellings were no more than patchwork shacks which seemed to have been carelessly erected from a few boards salvaged from some deserted settlement and whatever materials were at hand. Feeble and guttering lights showed behind the oil-paper windows.

As they neared the first shack, a door was opened and a man stepped into their path. 'That you, Lampasas? Who's with you?'

'Me all right. Posse was chasing this fella . . .'

'Heard the shooting. Thought you were practicing.' The man stepped nearer to them, sizing Kingdom up; a small young man with

94

the dark beauty of Lucifer. His black and merry eyes held a lively thrust of friendly curiosity. Somewhere, Kingdom thought suddenly, he had seen those eyes before, and not long ago . . .

'I'm Tory Stark,' the young man said, as though this were supposed to mean something. To Kingdom, it didn't, but the meaning was all there to read in the manner the fellow carried the heavy gun at his left side . . .

'Hello,' Kingdom murmured.

Tory laughed. 'A man of few words. I like that . . . I haven't seen you somewhere now, have I?'

Kingdom shrugged. He had heard this question somewhere before too, and could not think where. Then it came to him—the young stage robber he had shot had put these same words to him. And he knew with mild amazement that that man's eyes were those of which Tory's so strongly reminded him; in general features and build they were much alike too.

He had no time to consider the implications of this. Tory said, 'Taking him to Incham?' Lampasas nodded.

'I think I'll go with you,' Tory Stark said, 'for laughs.'

With Lampasas Teal leading and Tory bringing up the rear, they walked on down the footpath to the last shack, set just beyond a clump of cottonwoods.

Lampasas stepped by the door; he looked at Kingdom. 'Just one thing. Don't get mad.'

'At who?'

'Him. Just don't get mad.'

Lampasas knocked at the door.

'Who is it?'

'Lampasas.'

'Come in,' said the man inside, bored.

They stepped inside. He stood in his shirtsleeves with his back to them, shaving with the aid of a shard of mirror propped on two pegs driven into the wall. He said without turning, 'Close the door. What was the shooting?'

'Bunch of counter-jumpers were chasing a fella our way. I got rid of them. Brought the fella back with me.'

Incham unhurriedly finished shaving. Then he turned around, and looked Kingdom up and down. 'You're big,' he said casually. 'What're you running from?'

'What makes you think I'm running from anything?'

Incham sighed. 'You wouldn't be here if you weren't. So you were being chased ... By whom and why?'

Kingdom said nothing. Incham flung the towel aside and picked up his coat from a rickety chair, shrugging into it. He straddled the chair, leaning his arms on the back of it. 'That won't get you anywhere,' he said pleasantly. 'We don't have to be nice, you know. We can be just plain damn nasty and find out as much.'

The skin tightened and smoothed over Kingdom's Indian-high cheekbones. 'I don't think you can.'

Incham glanced at him shrewdly, one tawny sickle of an eyebrow lifting questioningly as though unaccustomed to such unco-operativeness. 'Damned if I don't think you're right. Only look at it this way.' Incham idly pulled a cigar from the breast pocket of his shirt and gestured absently with it. 'You come barging in here with a gang of town bums on your trail. For all we know you rigged it that way to jail our bunch. Just say you're a lawman—a United States Marshal or what-have-you—'

Incham smiled. 'Oh, yes, it could happen. Most of us are wanted as deserters by the Federal army, or,' he waved the cigar again, 'if we fought for the Lost Cause, for failing to report for parole. Bluebellies have put towns all over Texas under martial law. Putting the whole state under military government this year, so I hear ... The army's just part of it. Many people for other reasons would like to nail our hides up. Anyway, suppose you stay with us long enough to make sure of us, go back and lead a troop of cavalry in here.' Incham shrugged and smiled casually. 'You see how it is ...'

'A mob in Boundary was trying to lynch me.

That's all there is.'

'Ah—no, not quite. Why?'

'They thought I murdered a woman.'

Incham felt in his pockets and said mildly, 'Damn. Give me a match, will you, Tory?' He thoughtfuly poised the proffered match, glancing at Kingdom. 'Did you?'

'No.'

Incham regarded him silently for a long moment, then struck the match and held it to his cigar. 'I believe you. What's your name?' He chuckled then and the breath of it blew the match out. 'I mean to say,' he amended comfortably, 'what do you *call* yourself ...? Give me another match, Tory.'

Kingdom was silent as Incham lighted his cigar. Incham glanced at him and sighed, throwing the match away. 'All right. I'm John Incham ... Fair exchange?'

Kingdom was prompted to lie, but a wild and stubborn anger was carrying him now. To hell with him, he thought, and said aloud, 'Kingdom.'

He could hear a subtle outletting of breath from Lampasas at his elbow; before he had time to wonder at this, Tory said delightedly, 'Ha! I knew I'd seen you somewhere before! Dallas, sure! More than once ...'

For a moment, only a blank puzzlement was on Kingdom; then it came to him. These men thought he was Doug.

Kingdom had almost opened his mouth to

correct this when two thoughts came to him as one. One was that without their help, he was stranded on the desert on foot; he could not return to Boundary. The other was that he had no way of gauging the temper of these men. To give them the name of a nondescript would be to run a gantlet of suspicion which he was of no mind to court. But Doug Kingdom was a bedrock identity in the minds of these men . . .

So when Incham asked idly, 'Doug Kingdom?' he only nodded. 'In that event, welcome, Kingdom. You were of course looking for us as I surmised.'

'I heard about your place,' Kingdom lied. 'I only knew it was somewhere here.'

'Of course. And have you decided whether you want to become a part of us, or have you lone-wolfed it too long?'

It was an invitation, Kingdom knew, and he nodded. 'So long it got too rich for my blood. I like what I've seen of this place.'

'Good. Come over here tomorrow morning. I'd like to talk with you, explain a few things that will get us off to a concrete understanding ... You can stay with Lampasas. I doubt he'll mind the company of another lone wolf like himself.'

'That's what I had in mind,' Lampasas said in his easy Texan drawl.

'A good thing for you Lampasas likes to prowl around.' Incham smiled at Kingdom. 'You didn't leave anything behind in your expeditious departure, did you? Any luggage? We can get it for you.'

'It's all on my back,' Kingdom said, 'except my packhorse at the livery.'

Incham nodded. 'I'll have a man fetch it tomorrow ... I suggest we all retire early, gentlemen.'

It held the flat finality of a dismissal, and the three of them left Incham's shack, stepping into cottonwood-scented darkness. They walked in silence for a way.

'First time in years,' Kingdom mentioned, 'that I've been spanked and sent to bed.'

Tory laughed and slapped his thigh. Lampasas said dryly, 'Leastways he's considerate. He didn't tell us to get the hell out.'

'Not in as many words,' Kingdom said.

'Still, he's king here,' said Lampasas.

'And his word law,' Tory said merrily. 'You want to be nice to him, Brother Kingdom. Or he'll have me shoot you. And I kind of like you.'

Kingdom was on the point of letting that pass, then remembered the role he was playing—of boastful Doug ... 'You can always try,' he said calmly. He felt an inward shudder at Tory's answering laugh—like the laugh of the young stage robber; an underplay of winter chill through it ...

At Lampasas' shack they parted from Tory and went inside. Lampasas trimmed the wicks

100

of several beef-tallow candles. Lampasas' bed was a heap of springy boughs in one corner with some blankets thrown over them.

Kingdom spread his own bedroll on the floor, thinking that his one danger now lay in the possibility that someone in the gang had personally known Doug, though Lute had known Doug and had been at least partly deceived . . .

Kingdom did not trouble to look up from his blankets as the door behind him opened and someone hesitated on the threshold.

'What do you want?' he heard Lampasas say coldly.

'Just a candle. Just wanted to borrow a candle,' the man said.

Kingdom's hands froze on the blankets. That obsequious snivel—it could not be—and he turned his head to look, and it was Loomis all right . . .

Kingdom came off the floor on his hands and knees and before he was entirely on his feet was driving at Loomis. The little man saw him coming when Kingdom was almost on him; Loomis' mouth opened to scream and the scream never began because Kingdom hit him then with his fist—only once—and Loomis turned in his tracks and crashed face first into the wall. He began slipping to the floor like a tired child, and sprawled unmoving there.

Kingdom looked at Lampasas who was already staring at him. 'I don't like him either,'

Lampasas said at last. 'But what was that for?'

Kingdom gestured loosely toward Loomis. 'Ask him,' he said thinly.

'I think I better get Incham,' Lampasas said slowly.

'All right,' Kingdom said. Lampasas went out, and Kingdom, his breath labored with unexpended anger, stood looking bleakly down at Loomis and rubbing his knuckles. Incham came in followed by Lampasas. Tory was behind them; he stopped at the doorway and leaned there, grinning.

Incham looked down at Loomis, then glanced with an almost sleepy benignity at Kingdom. 'You must have had a reason for that.'

'I did. He did the job they were going to lynch me for.'

Incham looked more attentive. 'Woman-killing?'

Kingdom nodded.

'Well, well,' Incham said; he stared at Kingdom, rubbed his chin and looked down at Loomis. He bent down and slapped Loomis twice across the face. Loomis groaned and tried to fight him off. Incham slapped him again. 'Get up,' he said. 'So it was a woman you shot.'

'Wait—' Loomis said, slack-jawed.

'It was a woman,' Incham said gently. Loomis shut his jaws sullenly.

'You're under my protection or I'd let

102

Kingdom finish this,' Incham said. 'But get out tomorrow. I don't harbor woman-killers.'

Loomis stood looking at them, a small and helpless man seeming to shrink within himself even smaller, and even Kingdom could feel sorry for him in that moment. Moving slowly, like an old man, Loomis turned and walked from the room.

Incham turned to face Kingdom, saying apologetically, 'He rode in this morning wanting to join us. I laughed at him. He showed how scared he really was then. Started babbling about robbing a store and killing a man. I felt sorry for him, perhaps. At any rate, I said he could stay.'

'It was a rooming house he robbed,' Kingdom said, 'and shot the girl who owned it.'

'A brave play,' Incham said dryly, and added curiously, 'How did you happen to become embroiled?'

'I was seeing that girl some,' Kingdom said carefully. 'I happened to be in her place when this fella came in and tried to hold her up. She pulled a gun on him and he shot her and hit me a lucky blow with his gun and got away. The girl's brother found me holding the girl's gun with one bullet fired and thought I did it.'

Incham nodded thoughtfully. 'I heard you were seeing some girl in Boundary. Even heard you married her.'

'No. People talk.'

'And hens cackle,' Incham said. He smiled

103

faintly and slapped Kingdom on the arm, a gesture from this cold, remote man that surprised Kingdom. 'I'll see you in the morning,' Incham said, and left the shack. Tory grinned meaninglessly at Kingdom and Lampasas, and ambled silently out of the doorway and down toward his own shack.

Kingdom walked to the doorway and stood there watching Incham go, a small slight man with an erect and unconscious assumption of a big man's size. Kingdom rarely formed first judgement; when he did, they were tempered with a cautious reserve. Still, he thought that he liked Incham.

*　　　*　　　*

Tory Stark, in his shirtsleeves, eyes sleep-bleared, was frying bacon for his breakfast. He was lackadaisically turning it with a long fork while it spattered and bubbled in the skillet set on a bed of glowing embers in the bakedmud fireplace. A knock came at the door of his shack.

'It's open,' he growled, not troubling to rise from his squatting position before the fireplace. Dawn rarely found Tory in the ebullient humor which characterized him, especially after a nightly bout with a quart of Mountain Brook.

His humor was not improved when he saw that it was Loomis who stood at the threshold, fingering the reins of his saddled horse who stood patiently by, a bedroll lashed to the cantle.

'What do you want?'

'Talk,' Loomis said, his voice nearly inarticulate in the painful movement of his purple and swollen jaw.

Tory, forking his bacon out of the skillet onto a tin plate, eyed him with mild curiosity. 'What happened to you?'

Loomis told him with curses.

'That what you wanted to talk about?' Tory asked with mild amusement.

'No. I'm leaving now like Incham said.' A sly and malevolent gleam touched Loomis' red-rimmed eyes which betokened a painfully sleepless night. 'Only first I figured you'd like to hear about your brother's killer . . .'

Tory came upright and stalked wordlessly across to Loomis, doubling up the front of his shirt in one slim and trembling fist. 'You know?'

'Of course I know—I was on the stage that brought him in. Let go, dammit!'

Tory slowly released him and let his hand drop, staring at him. 'I remember. You were on the stage. You, the frog, his woman, the driver . . . Which of you was it?'

'None of us. It was the fourth passenger.' Loomis paused. He grinned, relishing this. 'Kingdom.'

Tory chuckled softly. 'It won't work, fella.

Kingdom wasn't on the stage. Like me to finish him for you, would you?'

'Damn it, he was on it! He left the stage before you saw your brother's body. Your brother held the stage up out of Boundary and Kingdom shot him in the back.'

Tory frowned; he recalled now that he'd seen a large man leaving the stage: it could have been Kingdom; the light had been poor, and he was not certain. Then he looked sharply at Loomis. 'You're a liar. His neck was broken.'

'Because Kingdom shot his horse and it threw him.'

Tory said thinly, 'Prove it.'

'Ask him! Go ahead, ask him!'

Tory threw his head back and laughed, long pure laughter rising clear and pealing in the still valley morning. 'He'd admit it, of course!'

'Why not?' Loomis said harshly. 'He's the kind of damn fool that would.'

Tory stopped laughing; he watched Loomis with a basilisk intensity. 'A man who would shoot at another man from the back is not the sort to admit it if admission would cost him his life.'

'The hell with you!' Loomis said wildly, beyond caution now. 'I'm giving you the name of the man. You don't want to do nothing about it, that's your damn business.'

He turned and stepped into his saddle and was violently turning his horse when Tory stepped through the door and grasped the reins. 'Just hold it,' Tory murmured. He squinted a little against the sunlight as he looked up at Loomis. 'There's an off chance this isn't a lousy saddle-bum trick. Yes ... I'll ask him about it. If he says you're a liar, I'll track you down and blow your damn head off. Understand? Now you get the hell out of here.'

Tory saw pleasurably the naked fear in Loomis' eyes as the little man wheeled the animal with a savage spurring down the footpath. Tory turned slowly, heavily, and stepped back into the cabin and over to the table, looking down unseeingly at the plate of bacon. With a sudden savage sweep of his forearm, he knocked the plate clattering to the floor. He stalked to the single rickety chair where his hat and coat and gunbelt hung. He clamped the hat on and buckled the gun on with sure, furious movements. Then he stepped out the door again, heading for Lampasas' shack.

CHAPTER NINE

Lute Danning hunkered on the ground before Incham's shack, his back propped comfortably against the wall, letting the drowsing coolness of the wakening morning and the warm early sunlight work through him while he lazily watched Incham, sitting on a bench by the door and talking.

He and Incham had spent most of yesterday discussing military tactics and their various applications. Incham was widely read as the well-worn and dog-eared volumes on the shelf inside testified.

And Incham was now on a subject upon which he so far scarcely touched—the most interesting of all, to Lute: the enigma that was Incham himself.

'I'm a tidewater Virginian, born and bred,' Incham said carelessly. 'I was in Richmond on business in sixty-two when McClellan's army was laying siege to it. When I got back to my plantation, I found it burned to the ground. My wife and daughter, they—' he broke off momentarily, staring at Lute who felt chilled, seeing the full blackness of memory tide back into his thoughts.

Incham's voice was bitter and toneless. 'Some deserters from McClellan's army, I judged. I found a blue kepi and a new Federal issue rifle on the scene. I never found the men. I just got a band of cutthroats and raided Yankee towns.'

Incham shifted restlessly and looked at Lute. 'I paid them back a hundred times over for my family and my home. I know now it wasn't the way. It wasn't the way at all. And after the war, it was too late . . .

'My men were fired upon by some drunken U.S. Cavalry when we came in to give our parole to the provost marshal. I reckon amnesty did not include bushwhackers. We were cut to pieces and scattered. Tory Stark is the only man of them still with me; he and I became tired of dodging Yankee patrols and came West . . . Ah! Here comes the fellow I was going to tell you about. Slipped my mind.'

Lute idly turned his head to look down the path at the man coming toward them.

Kingdom! Kingdom again! Lute thought in numbed disbelief. Then he caught on to Incham's words, glad that Incham had taken no notice of his agitation. Lute decided to play dumb, and see what would happen next.

'After you left for your shack last night,' Incham was explaining, 'Lampasas came to me with this fellow—said he'd been up on the rim when this fellow came riding up with a posse on his tail. Lampasas drove them off and brought the fellow to me. He said he hadn't been looking for us, but I suggested he stay. A cool customer. I think you'll like him.'

As Kingdom came up to them, his eyes rested only briefly on Lute before they shifted to Incham. Incham greeted him genially, inquired how he had slept, and motioned toward Lute. 'Lute Danning, Doug Kingdom.'

Kingdom acknowledged the introduction with a bare nod, the stern lines of his fresh-shaven face not relaxing. Lute's mind was whirling insensibly. So Kingdom was posing as his brother ... But this made no sense. What could Kingdom be after?

Kingdom absently hunkered down against the wall beside Lute, and began thoughtfully to build a cigarette. There seemed nothing to say, so Lute didn't comment.

'Quantrell,' Incham went on musingly, squinting at the sky. 'There was a fighter.'

'A killer,' Kingdom said quietly. Incham's gaze flicked back to Kingdom; he smiled ever so slightly. 'You're considering Lawrence, for example ...?'

'Over a hundred and eighty massacred,' Kingdom said quietly.

Incham snorted. 'Kansas freesoilers.'

'They were people.'

Incham regarded him closely, searchingly. 'You talk more like a damyank than a Southern bushwhacker.' His gaze strayed idly to Kingdom's Union Cavalry trousers. 'I don't know, you understand. I heard, just heard is all, that you were a guerrilla under Quantrell.'

Kingdom said coldly, 'You heard wrong,' as he stood up. 'If that's going to mark against me here—'

'Oh, sit down!' Incham said crossly. 'No one gives a damn who you fought for. I just want to talk ... I was curious; you sound like a Southerner.'

Kingdom said, 'I am,' warily.

'Ah,' Incham said, watching him shrewdly.

'Can a man ask why?'

'Matter of principle.'

'Oh, of course,' Incham mocked. 'Slavery issue . . .'

'I'm one of those damn fools who fought for what he believed,' Kingdom said without inflection. 'What did you fight for?'

Incham made a wry face, smiling. '*Touché*, Friend Kingdom. Still, it goes against the grain. I wrote back to Virginia recently and found they'd split my plantation up among a passel of negras. Can you blame a lot of Southerners for still fighting the war . . .? Dammit, Kingdom, you've ridden through Texas. What have *you* seen? Men coming home from the war to find their stock driven off or running wild, loose cattle roaming over a quarter million square miles, land-grabbing damyankee carpetbaggers, ex-Redlegs and Jayhawkers prowling the trails, hard-scrabble brushpoppers slapping a brand on everything with horns. It's no more than a step from mavericking to jayhawking. If men like us don't live as we do, we don't live. War's bitter legacy, Kingdom.'

'You might raise stock in a small way with all this unbranded stuff running loose.'

Incham shook his head moodily. 'We've got too many odds on us now.' He added with dry humor, 'Lute's the military expert here. Just full of ideas. On cattle stealing among other things. Only we'd need a market. Damn if I'd

111

care to try a Missouri drive . . .'

Kingdom said musingly, 'I was in Kansas City not long ago. Kansas Pacific Railroad is building through there to Denver. Talk was that a fellow named McCoy was starting a cattle-shipping center for Chicago at Mud Creek—stage station on the Butterfield Overland Line. They call it Abilene now. About a hundred fifty miles southwest of Kansas City. Cattle pens, stockyards . . .'

'Did you see these rails to Abilene?' Incham said skeptically.

'They'd gotten fifty miles west of Kansas City, almost to Topeka, last I heard. But they'd be to Abilene by this fall.'

Incham murmured, almost to himself, 'A Kansas drive . . . I wonder.'

'Army freighter named Jesse Chisholm said the herds could follow the trail left by his wagons, through the Nations, maybe to the Cimarron,' said Kingdom.

Incham spiraled out a stream of cigar smoke and considered all this in silence. Then he glanced suddenly at Kingdom. 'Now, there's an idea.'

'What?' asked Lute.

'There's a rancher out of Boundary—old Frenchy Santerre. He's got five thousand on the hoof and he'll drive to Nawleans in a week or less. Used to ranch on the Louisiana side of the Sabine. Moved to Texas during the war, built a new spread under his old Staghorn

112

brand. This'll be his first drive since the war ended.' Incham smiled at Kingdom. 'Do you like trail herding?'

'Why?'

'That'll be your job,' Incham said gently, speculatively. 'To get a job with Santerre for this drive. He's found it easy to get men for the roundup, but getting them to drive is another thing. Likely be short-handed and he'll be hiring. He'll hire you.'

'Why do I get a job with Santerre?'

Incham laughed. 'It'll be your task to persuade him to make a drive to Abilene—instead of Nawleans.'

Lute felt a mounting excitement as he listened to Incham say, 'And once the drive's under way, we raid him and take his damn herd off his hands—finish the drive ourselves and collect at railhead. And unless I miss the pattern, stock prices will be booming.'

'What's the difference between Louisiana and Texas?'

'I told you; Santerre shipped to Orleans before the war. His new brand's the same as the old; it'll be known in Orleans. The stockmen there know him; he always goes with his herds. What would happen if we tried selling his beef there?'

Kingdom was silent. Lute thought, He doesn't like it.

'You're new to these parts,' Incham went on. 'Santerre or some of his men know the rest of us by sight. It'll have to be you.'

'They don't know me,' Lute said.

'You're hardly built for trail driving,' Incham said dryly.

Lute felt a cutting anger at this unveiled gibe at his stoutness. Incham, ignoring him, said, 'Also, you had an argument with Santerre's foreman day before yesterday . . .'

Lute forgot his anger. 'Santerre's foreman? Hassard?'

'Yes, Hassard,' Incham said disgustedly. 'You'll have to be careful of him. So damn suspicious, his own wife hates him . . .'

'Anything else?' Kingdom asked dryly.

'Yes,' Incham grinned. 'There'll be a couple of women on Santerre's place, so keep your mind on the job . . . Hassard's wife—she's hell on wheels—and Santerre's daughter. Don't know anything about her; she just came to live there recently. She and her husband came in on the stage the other day—h'm, same one on which they brought in Tory's brother, remember, Lute?'

Lute felt an envious irritation. 'You know a hell of a lot about these people.'

Incham smiled and waved his cigar carelessly. 'I've had my eye on Santerre's herd for a long time—and I never go into anything blind. Drop a question here, a question there . . . Not hard.'

Lute glanced at Kingdom, who was staring at the ground, and Lute wondered what subtle

114

workings were going on behind his passive mask. Presently, to Lute's surprise, Kingdom said, 'I'll take the job.'

'Good,' said Incham. 'You can rest up today and head for Staghorn tomorrow. We'll thrash out the details between now and then . . .'

Tory Stark came striding up the path then, and watching him come, swinging along with the cockiness of a small man and the headstrong self-assurance of a big one, Lute had a sudden premonition of trouble.

Tory stopped before Kingdom and said very gently: 'Did you shoot a man whose body was brought in the stage day before yesterday, Kingdom?'

Kingdom regarded him deliberately. 'And if I did?'

'He was my brother . . .' In the dead stillness that hung over his words, Tory said softly, 'I asked you a question, Kingdom?'

Kingdom said matter-of-factly, 'When I'm shot at, I shoot back. He tried to rob us; he took his chances and lost.'

' . . . His life,' Tory said hotly.

'That was the stake and he paid it. Should have, too.'

'You *did* shoot at him from behind?'

Kingdom didn't reply for a moment. He looked down at his hands speculatively, then back at Tory and murmured, 'Loomis?'

'You shoot him in the back?' Tory demanded savagely.

115

'Shot at his back. Hit the horse.'

Tory shook his head in his wrath, as though baffled at finding this stolid integrity in a man who would backshoot.

Kingdom said: 'He shot at me first. When he started to get away, I got him.'

Tory let out his breath, settling his weight on his heels, watching Kingdom. 'Will you meet me?' Tory asked in a shaking voice.

'No.'

'Well, I'm not surprised,' Tory said with a deep malice. 'It would take a lot of nerve . . .'

'You're a fool, Tory,' Incham said, yawning. 'He's not afraid of you.'

Tory swung on him blazingly. 'Then why won't he meet me?'

'For the same reason no one would give a loaded gun to a baby,' said Incham in a hard low voice. 'Now hear me, Tory—I'll have no trouble in this camp. We need Kingdom, and your damn brother got his coming-up . . . Get out!'

Tory spoke to Incham, but it was at Kingdom that he looked. 'I don't like being baited, Mr. Incham. This isn't finished. Remember it.'

'We'll try to remember,' Incham said dryly.

Tory spun on his heel and stalked away, a dark little shape of menace.

Incham said lazily, 'He meant it, you know, Kingdom. He isn't finished and not even I can stop him. If the whim strikes him, he'll kill

116

without reason, and now he has a reason. He has only one answer to anything, living by the gun . . .'

'One of these days he's going to die by it,' Kingdom said.

'Quite,' Incham said moodily. 'The war taught Tory to place a shallow premium on human life. All I ask is, don't hate him. He can't help the way he is.'

'I don't hate a fool,' Kingdom said shortly.

Incham dropped his cigar butt and thoughtfully ground a heel on it. 'So you shot Tory's brother? Then you must have been on the stage with Santerre's daughter and son-in-law.'

'I kept them from being robbed.'

'Just what I was thinking. And Frenchy should be duly grateful to the man who helped them. Yes, he'll be glad to give you a job, Kingdom . . .'

Kingdom said nothing to that. He stood up, grinding out his cigarette against the wall; said, 'I'll be seeing if Lampasas has breakfast ready,' and walked back down the path.

As he disappeared among the trees, Incham turned to Lute. 'What do you think?'

'A good man,' Lute said cautiously.

'I was thinking so, yes,' Incham mused. 'Too good, maybe, for this game. A quiet man, with the look of an honest one. No judging by looks of course, but somehow he doesn't fit his reputation. Still, I like him—perhaps for that

117

reason.'

'So do I,' Lute admitted.

The conversation became desultory, and Lute took his leave for his own shack, one of Incham's well-worn volumes under his arm, anticipating a pleasant forenoon of reading. Heading down a sycamore-shaded footpath, he stopped abruptly, seeing the mirror-still surface of the stream ahead through a screening of bushes and Kingdom on the bank dipping up a bucketful of water.

Lute hesitated, having no inkling of the man's temper or intentions. For a moment he stood irresolute, then thought, The hell with it. I'll face him out. He stood, watching Kingdom straighten, come to his feet, and start back up the path to Lampasas' shack, the bucket of water swinging at his side. Then, stepping around a crook of the path, he saw Lute and came to a dead stop. Lute could see his fist gently tighten on the bucket handle; he gave no other hint of expression, only stood and silently watched Lute.

'I'm not looking for trouble, Kingdom,' Lute said in a dry voice.

'You found it, seems,' Kingdom said. His voice was chilled and dogged, every word distinct and spaced.

'Think back some, will you?' Lute paused, and when Kingdom said nothing, only waited grimly, Lute said: 'I could have brought you down after you shot DeRoso. I could have shot you in the back a minute ago . . .'

Kingdom still said nothing, and Lute said angrily, 'Damn it, I liked Doug.'

Kingdom said with the bite of a cold wrath, 'You had a damn odd way of showing it, friend.'

'All right,' Lute said angrily, 'I was going to trade on his name, and what of it? He was as tired of this life as I was. If a man sees maybe the one chance out of it, he'll take it. What happened, it was an accident—I'm sorry about that . . .'

'You're sorry. That will make my brother feel very well.'

'Dammit, it wasn't as though I pulled that trigger . . .! The worse thing I did was wanting to make some money.'

'If it meant spreading Doug's name across every wanted poster in the West.'

'Listen, once we had a stake we could have gone to South America maybe, maybe up to Canada. Canada. There's a nice peaceful country . . .'

Kingdom was shaking his head before Lute was done. 'You're finished, Lute. You don't know it, but you're finished.'

'Not by you, though. You make a pass at me, and Incham—'

'Yes, Incham,' Kingdom broke in. 'Going to use him the way you would have used Doug?'

Lute smiled with no humor. 'No one "uses" Incham—but you'll know that before long . . .'

'I'm not interested,' Kingdom said coldly.

'You come here looking for me?'

'Not for you, Lute. But I'll be seeing you . . . Now step out of the way.'

Lute moved out of the path and Kingdom walked by him without another glance at him. Lute sighed and was about to go on to his shack when he heard Tory Stark's voice so close at hand and so sudden that it unnerved him; Lute froze in his tracks.

'Stop there, Kingdom!'

Lute gingerly parted some twigs without exposing himself. He saw that Kingdom had come to a dead stop, facing Tory Stark who stood squarely athwart the path. Tory was smiling over the sun-glinting pistol poised negligently before him.

'I said it wasn't finished, Kingdom—drop the bucket.'

Kingdom dropped it; it struck the ground woodenly, tilted over on its side. The only movement for a long moment was the water runneling muddily back down the trail, long wet serpents creeping to coil into little hollows and distend in small gleaming pools . . .

It was Kingdom who broke the nerve-strung silence. 'What about Incham?'

'I can handle Incham,' Tory smiled. 'This is my affair and none of Incham's mix . . . Where's your gun?'

'In Lampasas' . . .'

'We'll get it, then,' said Tory, and stepped

off the trail, motioning Kingdom to move on ahead of him, then swinging into step behind.

It was then that Lute made his decision and moved. Pulling his gun, he eased out silently into the path and said sharply, 'Stand still, Tory, and drop it.'

Tory came stock-still, and for a moment in which Lute's breath hung still in his lungs he wondered if Tory would obey . . .

He did not drop the gun or turn—only spoke without looking around. 'We ain't been bad friends to now, Lute. Don't mess it.'

'Tory, I'm telling you, drop it . . . That's better. That's fine. Now walk away. Incham needn't hear a word of it.'

'You haven't heard the last of it,' Tory said meagerly, 'what's more important,' and was out of sight down the path.

Lute holstered his pistol and walked heavily on to meet Kingdom who had bent down to pick up Tory's gun. Without expression he handed it to Lute. 'I'll give it back to him when he's ready to behave,' Lute said. ' . . . How does the Dry Springs incident set now?'

'It's not forgotten,' Kingdom said shortly.

Lute could no longer fetter his curiosity. 'Why're you here? Why'd you agree to handle the Staghorn thing?'

'You're damn chatty for changing the subject.'

A sudden anger flared in Lute; his patience was gone.

'The hell with you!' he said wrathfully. 'I was Doug's friend. I want to be yours. But you make it so damn almighty hard for a man to like you with that sulky bear way you got to you—' He broke off, shaking his head in a baffled way. 'I still like you and damned if I know why . . .'

Lute turned violently and headed for his shack.

CHAPTER TEN

Even before a pastel dawn-flush softened the raw outlines of the Staghorn main house and outbuildings set comfortably in the gently rolling vale, Emilion DeLorme was down at his slope-roofed blacksmith shed, hammering with his sledge at a wagon felloe. When true dawn did come, Emilion, with a deep appreciation of these things, left his anvil, filled his stubby, blackened pipe, and stood watching the roseate firstlight seep across the land.

Full dawn was on the earth now, bright and clear and sharp, and Emilion threw back his gray-shot thickly black mane of hair with a toss of his leonine head and filled his great chest with the clean early air. Looking down toward the cookshack, he saw with no surprise that Wanda, in a faded crinoline dress, was already up with the dawn, moving between the rows of the cook's scanty garden with a rapt and childlike attention. Emilion's weather-troughed face softened a little . . .

She had seen him now and came lightly up the incline to his workshed. The young sunlight ran a fitful auburn tracery through her dark cheshnut hair, caught the light dust-spangling of freckles across her nose, and (ran Emilion's thoughts) danced in eyes which were the tranquil infinity of a summer dusk . . .

Wanda came to his side, her smile warm for him, and was about to speak when her glance fell toward the house. 'Look,' she said. 'There's Inez. Inez!' She waved to the tall woman who had just stepped onto the back veranda.

'*Sacre*, that termagant,' muttered Emilion.

Wanda protested. 'Why, she's lovely.'

Emilion was too French not to admit that Wanda was unquestionably right; Inez Hassard was beautiful of both face and form, even though *enceinte*, heavy with child, as now. A complexion, Emilion thought, as warm and clear as a summer sky, hair like ripe grain, eyes as gray as morning mist, a tongue edged like acid, and—occasionally—the temper of a thousand devils. Hassard had brought her to the ranch nearly a year ago. *Le Bon Dieu* only knew what she had been before that.

Hassard and she—they are a prize pair, Emilion thought sardonically.

123

Inez reached them, even this slight climb an obvious exertion to her. Sweat brightened her upper lip; her eyes were dark-circled. And not from too little sleep, Emilion thought disgustedly. *Ma foi*! but it was strange that the iron-handed Hassard made no effort whatever to regulate his wife in the way he did all else— or at least to hide her bottle. Not that, being married to that *cochon*, she was entirely to blame . . .

'You are up early,' Emilion said slyly.

She shielded her eyes from the sun, as though it hurt them. 'You're altogether humorous this morning, Emilion,' she said tiredly.

'You shouldn't have walked up here,' Wanda said, watching Inez' face anxiously.

'What's the difference,' she said tonelessly. 'If I could sit down—'

Emilion swept out a crate from behind the forge and placed it against the shed wall with a flourish. Inez sank onto it, putting her back to the wall and closing her eyes without thanking him.

Emilion restoked his pipe. 'The small one comes soon?' he asked conversationally.

Her eyes opened, the sudden gray of them pouncing on him. She looked down with distaste at her body. 'What do you think?' she said irritably. Wanda looked embarrassed; Emilion unconcernedly lighted his pipe.

'A baby,' Wanda smiled in her little-girl way

at Inez.

'I'll cut it out and give it to you,' Inez said, her face settling into a cast of utter bitterness.

'Inez!' Wanda had met Inez only two days ago; she could not yet reconcile the shocking venom of this beautiful woman's speech to her appearance.

'It's *his*,' Inez said tonelessly. 'I am bearing *his* child . . .'

'But to say—' Wanda faltered.

Inez looked at her slowly; to Emilion's surprise, her face gentled inexplicably as she watched the younger girl.

'Forgive me, my dear. You don't understand. Sometimes'—she sighed—'I wonder if I do.'

Emilion's brooding gaze roved out lazily to the heat shimmering plain beyond, then snapped to sudden attentive focus on a distance-tiny rider. He watched the horse-backer come nearer, wondering idly what the man's errand was at this early hour. Wanda and Inez presently followed his gaze, watching in silence.

Not long afterward, the stranger reined his blaze-face sorrel down in by the harness shed fifty yards distant and looked about the deserted ranchyard.

'I wonder what he wants!' Wanda murmured.

Emilion's voice lifted in a mild bellow. 'Ho, friend! You are looking for someone?'

The man's head swiveled swiftly, his gaze moving up the slight incline to the smithy's shed. He pulled his horse around and rode up toward them. Emilion's eyes widened in astonishment as he came nearer. Name of a name, but here was a man. He was fully as great through the chest and shoulders as Emilion himself, and inches taller. Emilion measured his face as well; it was somber and forbidding, with a be-damned-to-you look walled behind a still, black reserve.

Emilion's fingers began to twitch with a primitive excitement as he measured the lofty stranger's girth against his own. '*Sacre bleu*!' he murmured happily, the light of battle in his eyes.

The stranger, dismounting, heard him and his glance was unfriendly. The temper of him was edgy to the eye of Emilion. Then he heard Wanda say, 'Why, Mr. Davis!' in a tone of welcome that caused Inez' eyebrows to arch gently and made Emilion nod sagely and smile thoughtfully. There was more to this than the eye met.

'I knew I'd seen you before, sir!' Wanda said, extending her hand. 'Even with the change, I knew it!'

The stranger took her hand gingerly and gave a faint reluctant smile as though her delight were infectious to even his black mood. He said, 'You saw me before? With fur maybe?' He rubbed his clean-shaven chin.

'Yes,' she laughed. 'Yes Mr. Davis. With fur. Lots of fur.' She turned swiftly to Emilion. 'Oh, Emilion—this is the man I told about— who saved Jean-Paul's money on the stage . . . Mrs. Hassard, Mr. DeLorme—Mr. Jefferson Davis . . .'

'Jefferson Davis!' said Inez with a slow smile.

'That's what he told me,' Wanda said merrily.

'So *he* is the man!' said Emilion delightedly, his great hands closing and unclosing. 'Ah, *mais oui*, a fighter, this one! Ah, *joi* . . .!'

'Oh, Emilion,' Wanda said.

The stranger settled a cold and appraising look on Emilion.

'What, my friend,' inquired Emilion, hugely grinning, 'is your true name, seeing that the other must be a *nom de guerre*?'

The stranger looked Emilion over with great care. 'That,' he said very gently, 'is none of your business.'

Emilion's delight heightened. '*Nom de Dieu!* You do not disappoint me!'

'Stop it, Emilion,' Wanda scolded. 'Shake hands with Mr. Kingdom.'

'Kingdom?' Emilion scratched his head. 'That is a name?'

The stranger smiled faintly. 'It's not a common one,' he said, 'but this time it's real.'

Emilion swept out a hand, grinning wickedly. 'Pardon, M'sieu Kingdom.' Kingdom

127

regarded the hand for a long moment in a neutral way, then took it.

They struck hands and Emilion felt the stranger's hand tighten under the bone-crushing grip he deliberately applied. For a moment they strained and there was no perceptible give on either side. Only Emilion's smile faded slowly to a look of mounting puzzlement and slow-dawning bewilderment; Kingdom's face was expressionless.

'By gar, end it!' Emilion said suddenly, and they broke free. 'Brother,' Emilion said in awe, 'you should watch your strength. To this day, no one made Emilion DeLorme cry quit.'

Kingdom gingerly massaged his right hand, regarding Emilion with a grudging respect. 'You hadn't, I would.'

'If you're through making muscles, Emilion,' Inez said sweetly, 'let's not delay Mr. Kingdom's business any longer.'

'I'm sorry,' Wanda said, laughing. 'Do you have business here, Mr. Kingdom?'

'I was looking for a job,' Kingdom said. 'Heard you were starting a drive in a few days.'

'Why, Father said he had all the men he needs, but—oh, surely he can find a place for you . . . Come, he should be at breakfast.'

She set off down the incline with Kingdom, he leading his horse. Emilion, curious, knocked out his pipe against the forge and started after them. He paused by where Inez sat and extended an arm to her with the finesse of a courtier of Old France. She hesitated, unaccustomed to such courtesy, then nodded her thanks and stood with his help. Afterward, they followed Kingdom and Wanda to the veranda of the rambling house of hand-hewn timbers. Etienne Santerre himself had just stepped out the back door as Emilion and Inez reached it.

Seeing Santerre, Emilion felt his customary swell of inward pride that he worked for this tall, imperial-looking man. Like Emilion, of French-Canadian extract, Santerre was an exceedingly distinguished picture of a man, his coal-black hair and trim, precisely clipped Vandyke set off by threads of gray above the temples. His kindly eyes were the dark violet of Wanda's. Yet he affected nothing; he dressed as shabbily as the sorriest man of his crew in homespun jeans and a much-washed linsey-woolsey shirt with an old-fashioned stock, once white but now a dishrag gray. His one concession to dignity was a clawhammer coat, rusty-black with age.

'Father, this is the man of whom I told you—from the stage—Mr. Kingdom.'

Santerre came off the veranda. He did not embrace Kingdom or kiss him on the cheeks; he grasped his hand and measured him with cool eyes that saw much. '*Mon ami*, you saved my son-in-law's bankroll, so I understand. I am in your debt for any favor you may request.'

'All I'll ask you for is a job,' Kingdom said.

Santerre raised a finger and smoothed the point of his beard thoughtfully. 'You have struck me for the initial favor at shall we say an unpropitious time, monsieur. I have in very fact as many men as I require for the trail drive. For you, however, I think we can use an extra hand.'

Kingdom thanked him.

'My son-in-law is ill abed,' Santerre said. 'The tedious days on the stage ... He would be glad to see you, I know ... Have you breakfasted yet ...? No ...? Then please join us in the kitchen. You will want to wash up, of course; the wash bench is at the back ... The corrals are beyond.'

Emilion, more or less a privileged character on the ranch, ate with the family, together with Hassard and his wife, as often as he ate with the crew, and he followed the others into the kitchen, pausing at the door to watch Kingdom leading his horse up to the corrals. Him I must fight at all costs, Emilion thought contentedly, knowing that he would know no satisfaction until he had matched his strength against Kingdom's.

'Julio! Set the table,' Santerre called. 'Set an extra place. Sit down, my children ... Is your husband up, my dear?' he asked Inez.

'I'd hardly know,' she said indifferently, sinking listlessly into the chair Emilion held for her. Santerre looked at the table, somewhat embarrassed, doubtless recalling that Mr. and Mrs. Hassard did not sleep in even the same part of the house.

The house cook, a slender Mexican boy, had set the places and was bringing in the food when Hassard appeared in the doorway leading off the kitchen to the sleeping quarters. His eyes were bloodshot; he was unshaven and shirtless, his cotton underwear, above his trousers, dirty. 'Breakfast already? Can't you wake a man?'

'That might be possible,' Inez said tartly, 'if you'd tuck your bottle in a separate bed nights.'

Hassard laughed. 'Oh Lord, listen to that! The blind leading the blind.'

'You don't see me groaning about waking up, do you?' she snapped.

Hassard snorted. 'I don't see you drinking out of a teacup evenings, either.'

'Bless you,' Inez told him.

Emilion roared and banged a fist on the table, saying, 'Family felicity, by gar, amity and accord!' being very proud of his command of words, and never losing a chance to demonstrate it.

Santerre rapped a spoon sharply against his coffee cup. 'Enough! We are civilized human beings, not barbarians. Eat; be silent.'

Hassard pulled a chair out from the table, scowling blackly, and had begun to sit down when Kingdom came through the back door into the kitchen. Hassard stopped in

131

midmovement as though turned to rock, his eyes on Kingdom. A tremor shook Hassard; he caught at his belt for a gun which he recalled too late wasn't there.

'Oh for heaven's sake!' Inez said in exasperation. 'Now what?'

Hassard looked wildly about; he saw the heavy Sharps buffalo gun mounted on its pegs on the wall behind Emilion's chair and lunged around the table after it. Emilion leisurely, effortlessly swung a leg in front of Hassard as he came past Emilion's chair, tripped him, and sent him sprawling headlong. Emilion reached up then and plucked the rifle from the wall, turning it in his hands judiciously.

'You wanted this, m'sieu,' he observed innocently to Hassard. 'But why? Is it perhaps that you perceived a snake?'

Hassard got up slowly. He said, his face white with rage, 'I'll remember this, DeLorme.'

'I did not intend that you should forget it, m'sieu,' Emilion said smoothly, giving Hassard his most beamingly tranquil smile. 'But come. Apprise us of the reason for this display of truculence.'

'Yes, the reason, Egan,' Santerre said sharply. 'Mr. Kingdom is a guest under our roof, and as such is immune to unwarranted acts of violence. You have shamed us with this; now, explain yourself.'

The words dragged thickly from Hassard's

tongue. 'Ask him. He shot my sister two nights ago ... Killed her ...' The last words tore from him in a violent whisper.

Every eye swiveled to Kingdom who stood in the doorway, watching Hassard with a guarded wariness.

'Why did I not hear of this?' Santerre said angrily.

'You might have asked me,' said Inez wearily. 'I've heard little else for two days. He came in drunk the other morning and harangued me for hours about it. All he'd say was some gunman shot Melanie. I couldn't get more out of him.'

Wanda said coldly, 'He had to have a scapegoat on whom to fix the killing, and chose Kingdom.'

'Mr. Kingdom,' Santerre said quietly, 'you owe us a word.'

'I'll tell—' Hassard said thickly.

'Be quiet, Egan,' Santerre said. 'Let Kingdom speak.'

Kingdom let his breath out slowly. 'I came West to look for my brother after the war ended. He'd ridden with Quantrell and had been outlawed. I followed him to a town north of here. He was shot by a trigger-happy boy and died telling me about his wife here in Boundary. I came here to tell his wife of his death. She was Hassard's sister ... While I was talking to her in her house, a tramp broke in and demanded money. She pulled a gun on the tramp and he shot her. Hassard came in, found me there, and blamed me for the killing.'

'But what of the man who committed the crime—the tramp?' demanded Santerre.

'No one saw him,' snapped Hassard. He glanced at Kingdom, his voice edged with hateful mockery. 'No one—except Kingdom . . .' He added wickedly to Kingdom, 'How are your friends?'

Emilion watched the big man stiffen all over. 'My friends?'

'Yes! The ones who shot at us and drove us off when we caught up with you the other night . . .'

'You're mistaken,' Kingdom said gently. 'I was the only one shooting at you.'

Santerre said in a puzzled way, 'What of this?'

Hassard said hotly, 'I got some men and ran him out of town. We'd caught up to him and dehorsed him and he dodged into some chapparal. There was shooting then, and we were driven off.' He scowled. 'I don't know. I could've sworn someone besides him was shooting at us. Maybe not . . .'

Emilion guffawed. 'Hassard merely hates to admit he was driven off by one man! My congratulations, M'sieu Kingdom!'

Wanda said angrily, 'Ran him out of town, indeed! Tell about the lynching, Mr. Hassard! You forgot that!'

Hassard eyed her uneasily and looked away.

134

Santerre groaned softly. 'A lynching now! What else?'

'Let me tell you, Father,' Wanda said quickly. ' . . . Hassard incited a group of men to lynch Mr. Kingdom and shot at him on the street when he attempted to escape. Marshal Frost and his deputy helped him get away, but Hassard and his gang pursued him out of Boundary. That was the last I saw of them until Mr. Hassard came back hours later and drove Jean-Paul and me out to the ranch that night. He was drunk and quite offensive.'

'He's that first half the time and the last all the time,' Inez observed.

Santerre said wrathfully, 'Why did not you not tell me of this before, my dear?'

'I—did not want to make trouble for Hassard. But I could not stand now and let him condemn Mr. Kingdom.'

Santerre swung on Hassard. 'So! I wondered why it took you two days to bring my child and her husband to the ranch, Egan. Your excuse was thin, I thought, and I was right.'

Hassard watched Santerre; now that the die was cast, a kind of patient resignation had come to the segundo.

'Egan,' Santerre said in a surprisingly gentle voice, 'this is a bad thing. I have not heard you deny what has been said against you. But you have been a good man to me, and I wait for you to speak in your own defense.' When

Hassard said nothing, Santerre went on, still gently, 'Did it not occur to you, Egan, that were Kingdom truly your sister's killer, he would scarcely come seeking work at the ranch where you are segundo?'

Hassard said thickly, stubbornly, 'I put it down to gall. He came in here trading on the friendship of your daughter and her husband—maybe to wait for a chance to get back at me.'

Santerre smiled and gestured at Kingdom. 'Would a man so big be capable of something so small, Egan?' When Hassard was stubbornly silent, Santerre said tiredly, 'It would not be fair to discharge you, Egan. Your service has been good.'

'As a damn errand boy?'

Santerre's falcon gaze sharpened on him. 'I sent you after my daughter and her husband for the same reason I made you my segundo— you are my most trustworthy man. That is why I keep you now. Neither could I discharge you with your wife in her present state. But Kingdom stays. And if you stay, I must have your word that there will be no conflict between you.'

Hassard was silent so long that Emilion wondered if he would answer. He saw Hassard look at Kingdom and at Inez and back to Kingdom, finally to say tonelessly, bleakly, 'It won't be started by me.'

'Then the matter is closed,' Santerre said

with finality. 'We eat. Ho, Julio! More coffee.'

Kingdom and Hassard took their seats and began to eat without looking at each other. The silence over the table was constrained and tense. Emilion, bent over his plate, cast an occasional glance at Kingdom or Hassard.

The matter closed, he thought scornfully. *Voila*! but look at them. The match and the powder keg . . .

CHAPTER ELEVEN

Kingdom was down by the wagon shed where he had the spring wagon up on blocks, the wheels off, when the coming night forced him to quit work. He would finish tomorrow. He went up to the bunkhouse and cleaned up at the outside wash bench. He could hear the crew inside, bantering back and forth. Because it better suited his solitary nature, he walked away from the bunkhouse off into the quiet of the growing night toward Emilion's smithy.

He rolled a cigarette as he walked slowly, thinking—something he had assiduously avoided through hard work in the two days since he had come to Staghorn.

This is a fool's game, he thought. I should have kept on riding when I left the valley . . . But he had not, and Kingdom could not say why. And now he could not turn back.

Somehow he must find a way to help Santerre, whom he had come to like . . .

Kingdom paused by the rear of the house to light his cigarette. As its orange flare washed up in the cool dusk, and he bent his head to it, the door to the rear veranda opened, light falling softly into the yard. Mrs. Hassard stepped into the doorway. He came to a stop, hoping that she wouldn't see him in the poor light, but her silver tinkling laughter spilled into the night.

'Come over here, Kingdom. Come over here or I'll scream.' She waggled a finger at him. 'Better come. I could say you were molesting me and ol' Frenchy would have you horsewhipped off Staghorn . . . You don't think I'd do it?'

'I have no doubt you'd do it,' Kingdom said grimly.

'You are right,' she said in a grave and tipsy voice. 'A drunk will do anything. And I am drunk, Kingdom. Quite. Come over and help me sit down.'

He hesitated and she smiled warningly; he stepped over and assisted her to sit on the edge of the porch. 'You too,' she said. He sat down warily at a distance.

'Now,' Inez said, 'what is your opinion of me, Kingdom?'

'I had heard,' Kingdom said dryly, 'that you were hell on wheels, Mrs. Hassard. I believe it.'

She laughed genuinely. 'Who said that?'

'A man who loves beauty. Good night.'

'Oh, sit down ...!' Inez regarded him speculatively. 'You didn't come to this ranch for nothing . . . Was it to make trouble?'

He said warily, 'Why that?'

'Because you knew Egan would try to shoot you on sight. Knowing that, you had the gall to ride in here and touch old Frenchy for a job.'

Kingdom said carefully, 'I had no way of knowing that your husband was segundo here.'

Her lips half curved. 'I don't believe a word you're saying. I saw the way you looked at Egan the other day when you surprised him at breakfast. *You* weren't surprised. You were ready for trouble was all. And you looked it.'

'My reason?' Kingdom asked tightly.

'Reason? Oh, yes . . . Well, there's Wanda.'

His throat tightened; he started at her, his heart a pulsing drum roll in his ears. 'I—don't—'

'You needn't pretend, Kingdom,' Inez said carelessly. 'I've seen the way you look at her. I know you met her before you came to Staghorn. And she's why you came.'

'You're seeing things,' he said thinly.

'Am I then, Kingdom? But I couldn't be seeing things two-sided.' She laughed quietly. 'You see, she's been looking too. She's a very fine mother to her husband . . .'

'About her, you're wrong,' he heard himself say.

'You men make me sick!' Inez snapped. 'You shove us women up on pedestals and expect us to stand there all our lives like painted little puppets. You've built a nice pretty halo around her head, and it's going to fall off the first time she sneezes. Sure she's sweet and innocent, but still a woman. And if you don't walk in and take her away from him, you *are* a damned fool.'

'And what about him?' Kingdom asked dryly.

'Oh, stop trying to sound ironic, Kingdom. It fits you like a glove with ten fingers. He doesn't give a hoot about his wife as a wife . . . Don't look so surprised. Villon's a Creole gentleman, the last word in courtesy—But how many small attentions does he give her . . . ? Oh, he doesn't realize it. Not at all. Down in him, though, he thinks of Wanda as nothing but a backwoods girl, just a cornfed calico sweetheart. The sophistries of New Orleans society are under his skin, and for all he's a fine fellow, he doesn't give a damn for all the innocence in the world . . . '

She smiled faintly. 'Am I boring you, Kingdom? No . . . ? Well, that's about it. They shouldn't have been married. And she, at least, knows that.'

'Did she tell you?'

'She didn't have to.'

Kingdom said nothing; he felt with utter certainty that Wanda would never be disloyal to Villon, however mismated they were. Riding him still was that sense of wrongness.

'Actually, she's no more than a girl . . . much too young for you, Kingdom. But too young for Villon, for that matter . . .' She yawned, seeming to lose interest in the subject. 'I'm going to get a drink. Join me?'

Kingdom felt his brief rapport with her vanish. 'No.'

'Don't be righteous. You'd drink too, married to him.'

'It's not Hassard,' Kingdom said irritably. 'You drink because you're afraid.'

To his surprise, the smooth composure of her face crumpled and shrank. 'Don't say that,' she whispered. 'Don't ever say that. It's ugly.'

'Fear is seldom pretty,' said Kingdom wearily. 'I'm sorry.'

'No—you're right. It is my only reason; I really hate liquor. I've told myself for a long time I'll quit—now, perhaps I will . . .' She looked at him with a strange gentleness. 'Thank you, Kingdom. You're a big man in more than one way . . .'

'We'll forget that,' he said in a gruff voice.

She fingered a pleat in her skirt thoughtfully. 'Egan's a good man. He took me out of a job as gambling shill in El Paso and made me his wife. We could have been happy. But he tried to run me as he tried to run his sister Melanie, and it was no good. He has to twist and break everything he thinks he owns. I

141

wouldn't take that. One night he found me taking a sip of brandy and became violently angry.

'I understood then how I could best defy him—by drinking—so I did.'

'I think I understand.'

'I really think you do. Bless you for that, Kingdom.'

'Bless him?' said Hassard, so near at hand in the soot-black darkness of the yard that both started. He stepped into view in the lamplight then. Kingdom wondered how much he'd heard. He had been drinking; his step was unsteady. They watched him warily. 'Bless him?' Hassard said sardonically. 'Bless is not your customary term—not the one for me.'

'Oh, stop shooting at the sky, Egan,' Inez said disgustedly.

Hassard's gaze flicked to Kingdom. 'How did you get here?'

'I was able to walk.'

'You're a purple fool, Egan,' Inez said coldly. 'We were talking.'

'Just so, my dear ... About me. I want to talk to you, Kingdom.' He looked at his wife. 'Go inside.' She did not move. 'Go inside, I said!'

'I'd go, Mrs. Hassard,' Kingdom said quietly.

'I'd better.' She stood with Kingdom's help. She looked at Hassard then, her voice very clear. 'Don't worry for me, Kingdom. He

142

hasn't sunk to wife-beating—yet.'

She stepped into the house then, pulling the door to behind her, and the veranda was in complete darkness. Kingdom spoke into it: 'The matter deserves a thought before you jump.'

'Never mind that,' Hassard's voice said between his teeth. 'I long ago quit noticing what my wife does, and much less care.'

He's lying, Kingdom thought neutrally, and waited for him to go on.

'What I wanted to talk to you about,' said Hassard, 'was this drive.' A match flared in the darkness; he looked at Kingdom over the flame; and Hassard's face was suddenly wolfish in the wash of ruddy light. He lighted his cigar and threw the match away; the cigar tip bloomed brightly, cherry-red against sable night. 'You went to a peck of trouble to persuade the old man to make the drive north. Why?'

'Let's say I like progress.'

'Let's say something stinks. Why should you give a damn where we drive? Still, you do . . .'

'The market,' Kingdom murmured. 'Up to twenty dollars a head, maybe. Santerre did me a good turn hiring me when he had enough men. My turn.'

The disbelief in Hassard's voice carried to him in the darkness. 'Twenty dollars a—? Now I know you're lying,'

'You think so?'

'I don't believe the railroad's reached Abilene yet,' Hassard snapped, 'if there *is* a place called Abilene ... Let's say for the sake of argment there is—how far is it?'

'About a thousand miles. Up through the Cherokee Strip and the Nations. Good grass. Buffalo've foraged there for ages. So can cattle.'

'That's three months and more on the trail. And the Nations—border gangs, Indians, desert, floods, quicksand, Lord knows what. I don't like it ...'

'You're breaking me all up,' Kingdom murmured.

'That's not a bad idea!' Hassard snapped. His cigar was flung to the ground with a brief fiery arc and an angry shower of sparks in the night. 'I'm not done with you, Kingdom.'

'And your promise to Santerre?'

'That applied as far as the ranch.' Hassard's voice softened ... 'We'll be on the trail soon. A hundred days on the trail. A lot can happen in that time. A great deal can happen on a drive. Yes ... It can even happen to you, friend.'

Kingdom heard him turn, begin to walk away; then suddenly he came back. ' ... And by the way, Kingdom. There *was* someone in that chaparral the other night, shooting at us ... Someone besides you ...' Kingdom could hear the bitter smile in Hassard's voice. 'I recall now, I saw your dead horse. And your

144

rifle was still on the saddle; you didn't have time to take it with us almost on you. Well, whoever shot at us was using a rifle.'

Kingdom did not answer.

'So you have friends, Kingdom. And I'm wondering if that has anything to do with your being here . . . ? Sleep on it, Kingdom.'

With a laugh, Hassard walked off into the darkness.

And Kingdom did little sleeping.

CHAPTER TWELVE

Hassard stood in the cold half light of pre-dawn near the bunkhouse, rolling a dead cigar from one side to the other of his mouth, looking restlessly across the stirring hulk that was five thousand head of massed, horn-tossing cattle. Nearly gaunt, string-muscled cattle. Soup stock, Hassard thought contemptuously, and half wild, the lot.

Today, at any rate, the drive would begin. He could hear the shouts of the riders hazing the distant edges of the herd. Two ox carts had been drawn up before the bunkhouse, piled high with the warbags of the crew. Some of them were at work at a branding chute a hundred yards distant, searing the road brand into the last bunch of longhorns brought in.

Villon, in rough-jeans and a much-washed

shirt—a far cry now from the *bon mot* of New Orleans—was at the chute gate, working the bar that opened it. Kingdom held the running iron in gloved hands, drawing it now down a steer's flank. The beast bawled and lunged for the gate which Villon swiftly opened for it. Young Murray Ambergard waited there on his chestnut gelding, and he paused briefly to exchange a friendly word or two with Kingdom and Villon before he hazed the steer toward the herd.

Seeing Santerre coming down from the house, Hassard ground the cigar beneath his heel and walked to meet him.

'Really letting your son-in-law come on this drive, are you?'

'You object, Egan?'

'A drive is no place for a sick man.'

'He cannot become well by sitting at home. He wished to accompany this drive, and while he may well regret it later, I did not refuse. He can at least drive a wagon . . .'

Hassard sulked in silence and looked restlessly away, over toward the branding fire, whose smoke lifted and furled and was one with the thick dust as another steer went into the chute. One of the hands, Harve Soberin, had just come from breakfast, relieving Kingdom at the iron, and Kingdom went down to the cookshack for his own meal.

Hassard saw Villon's wife, a shawl thrown about her shoulders, stepping off the veranda

146

up by the house and coming on down toward the branding chute to speak with her husband. Hassard's mouth tightened. Inez would not do as much for him; she would not even be up by the time they left.

He saw with some puzzlement that Villon and his wife did not embrace, that there was great constraint in their parting, and he was wondering about this when Wanda left her husband and came over to where he and Santerre were standing.

'Have you seen Kingdom, *mon père*?' she asked. There was high, excited color to her cheeks. And not because she's cold, Hassard thought cynically.

'*Dieu de Dieu, mon enfant*—Kingdom! But I thought you would be desirous of spending these last moments of parting with your husband.'

She blushed deeply in a way that lofted Hassard's tawny eyebrows in sardonic speculation. 'Of course with Jean-Paul,' she murmured. 'But I want to say good-by to Kingdom. Where is he?'

Santerre said, regarding her with a deep trouble in his face, 'I saw him go to eat but a few moments ago.'

Taken shyly aback by what she saw in her father's face, Wanda said hurriedly, 'Thank you,' and walked toward the cookshack.

Watching her go, the troubled sadness grew weightier on Santerre's features. He was

147

French, and far from blind to the pattern that these things made. This thing that was coming to his daughter was very bad. All this Hassard could read in his face.

'Doesn't look so good, does it?' Hassard murmured.

Santerre settled a wintry gaze upon him. He said icily, 'I have never known Wanda to be indiscreet, Egan. And I advise you to look to more discretion in your own actions—and speech.'

Hassard smiled with great thoughtfulness. He did not reply.

*   *   *

Sheep Dip, the cook, complained stormily as he left off packing grub and utensils in his wagon to dish up food for Kingdom—beans, biscuits, and coffee which he had been keeping warm in the cookshack for the crew's morning meal. He was a small, balding and unshaven man who, in the fierce tradition of trail chefs, found an excuse for irascibility in the most minor awry detail. Kingdom knew it to be his apex of contentment and turned a deaf ear to it as he carried his food to the long table while Sheep Dip, cursing him bitterly, stormed back out to his wagon to finish loading.

Kingdom was alone now and he ate slowly, with the solid content of a man of solitary nature. The door opened at his back and he glanced over his shoulder to see Wanda there. He came to his feet, almost spilling his coffee.

'Please sit down,' she said. 'If I bother you—'

'Why should you?'

Some determination fought with her shyness. 'Because you really like to be alone—don't you?'

'I would reckon so, but it's only a habit.'

'No. It's a part of you. It really is. You're a quite complete man. Kingdom. Sufficient unto yourself.'

'Not that complete. Like saying a man can't be lonely.'

Her violet eyes widened. 'You, lonely? You, Kingdom?'

A heavily self-conscious embarrassment swept him and he thought with anger, How did we get off on this? This personal talk must be guarded. His feelings were deep-buried; he would keep them so. He said patiently, as to a child, 'You would not understand.'

'Perhaps.'

'No.'

'That is to say that a woman can't be lonely.'

'You have a man,' he said roughly.

He was surprised by the fleeting shade of pain crossing her face. 'Perhaps,' she said, 'perhaps you think I am lying to sympathize with you.'

Kingdom let his breath out tiredly. 'It's too bad you're not,' he said. 'Only you're not. No one lies about being lonely.'

Her head was tilted back to watch his face; her eyes dilated briefly, and she looked away from him. She said, 'Good-by,' almost inaudibly, and was out the door at the same moment.

Kingdom settled on the bench to finish his breakfast, and could not finish. He washed down most of what remained with his coffee and stepped outside as a crewman's bawl lifted into the rose-pearl dawn: 'We're moving!'

Kingdom hurried to the corral where some hands were assembling a picked remuda of nearly three hundred of the countless lean mustangs which grazed Staghorn range: cutters, ropers, broncs. Wrangler Porfirio Montoya, a dashing Mexican youth in greasy buckskin *chivarras* and an ornate charro jacket, cursed enthusiastically horses and men alike in the tongue of his fathers as he rode back and forth, bunching the remuda, in which, somewhere, was the blazeface sorrel Incham had given Kingdom.

He asked Porfirio for a horse. Porfirio cursed him and cut him out a mount. Kingdom saddled up at the harness shed; he was placed in the drag with the green riders by a curt word from Hassard.

Santerre sat his horse by Hassard, his dark eyes roving the faintly stirring bulk of the herd. He looked at his riders at their postions; he raised his arm and let it fall.

'Yip-yip-yeeowee!' This was the rebel cry

150

from the drag that set the herd in motion. An imperceptible movement at first, beginning around the outer periphery of it. It swelled and moved; it seemed to breathe, as though a couchant monster with an integrated life of its own. The cry was taken up. Irresistibly, the herd shifted north.

The drive had begun.

Hassard and Reeves Gayland, on point, swung the lead steers out, lining them at the end of a slowly forming crescent, guided and built by flankers and swing men. The cattle assumed the form of a strung-out trail herd five hundred yards in breadth, an immensity of life shaped by the prompting of thirty riders.

Sullen dustclouds billowed chokingly about the drag-riders in the wake. Through the haze, Kingdom could see the others assigned to the drag. He knew a few by name: Breen, the drag-boss; Granger, Lovelace; and off to his left, young Murray Ambergard, dwarfed in his mackinaw and barrel-leg chaps. Murray saw him now and grinned whitely through the shrouding dust-pall: 'Hi-hah, dust-eater!' Kingdom lifted a hand in reply and headed in to cut off a mulberry steer who had angled back among the stragglers.

He had leisure now to wonder when Incham would strike. He would follow with his crew of human scavengers ... and wait ... and wait. Kingdom had had no opportunity to take a count of Incham's men back in the valley, but he guessed them to be ten or a dozen. Even outnumbered three to one, a formidable handful in a surprise attack. Incham had said he would warn Kingdom before the raid and apprise him of his part in it. He must make his plans to help Santerre pending that warning . . .

CHAPTER THIRTEEN

Night camp was made on suitable bed-grounds near a grove of the scrub oak called blackjack. A thick ground fog gathered through the ocean of night, becoming ruddy-misted about the campfire, a half-mile from the bed-grounds. The men sat about the fire, wolfing their grub and too tired for much talk. Santerre was pushing hard these first days to make the herd trail-wise swiftly.

Porfirio, scheming how to break the apathy, walked with his empty plate and cup over to the wreck pan on Sheep Dip's wagon and dropped the dishes with a clatter that made everyone look up.

Porfirio winked at them, then looked soberly at the cook. 'Sheep Dip, boy, know what we need?'

Sheep Dip paused suspiciously in the act of loading a plate for himself. 'What?'

Porfirio delicately picked his teeth with the

tip of his Bowie knife. 'We need a cook.'

Sheep Dip used bad language. There were grins; this was life's own spice to cook and crew alike. Sheep Dip damn well knew how to cook with the best, he said; he had been twenty years practicing.

'What did he say?' yawned Lovelace.

'He said he's been practicing spoiling grub for twenty years,' Porfirio said tranquilly.

'No wonder he's so damn handy at it,' said young Overmile.

'He ain't practicing on us,' said Lovelace. 'Get a rope.'

'Let's have him fight Emilion,' said Granger.

'Bah, I fight big game,' said Emilion. His gaze settled slyly on Kingdom. 'Like him.'

'Fight him, then—fight Kingdom.' They took up these words and passed them about.

'*Regardez*,' boomed Emilion. 'He sits; he does not speak.'

'Man's taken with himself, isn't he?' Kingdom murmured.

'Ha? You fight?' Emilion asked, grinning, his hands twitching.

'Do you want an engraved invitation?' Kingdom asked dryly.

A ripple of talk ran over the group; they cleared a space in the pool of firelight. Despite the chill, Emilion and Kingdom flung off coats and shirts and rolled the top of their underwear down tightly around their waists.

'Boots too,' Emilion said. 'We wrestle—eh?'

Kingdom was no wrestler, and he suspected that Emilion knew it; still, he nodded and pulled his boots off. The men murmured; they made bets. Another fight might have been only a pleasurable break in the monotony of the trail, but this . . .

They began to circle in, arms half before them, hands poised. The soft wash of firelight set their thickly muscle-coiled upper bodies palely agleam, the deep brown of face and hands startling by contrast. Emilion's Indian-dark eyes danced with the purest of happiness.

Kingdom would not strike first; he waited for Emilion to make the opening move. Emilion was very patient. He kept Kingdom circling for a full minute, then sprang in, his right hand closing over Kingdom's left shoulder. Emilion tried to close, but Kingdom wanted to avoid closing. He ducked under Emilion's arm, and when Emilion tried to lock his neck, he lifted his shoulder into Emilion's belly and heaved massively. Emilion nearly left his feet, then caught his balance. More warily now, he circled again.

Emilion grabbed at his shoulder again. This time Kingdom could not avoid closing, and they strained powerfully together. For the first time, Kingdom felt fully the awesome strength of the man. Then he let Emilion hook a leg around his left one and throw his weight into him. To keep his feet, Kingdom instinctively tried to fling his left leg back for support, found too late that the leg was immobilized by Emilion; and the blacksmith's weight carried him backward and onto the ground, the breath driving from him with the impact.

Emilion sat on him, beat his arms aside, and caught his throat. Emilion's fingers tightened powerfully; Kingdom, his wind already broken, found Emilion's strength resistless. He fought to break the hold, and with all his effort, could not. Then some boyhood wrestling trick came to him. He wedged his fingers beneath Emilion's thumbs and twisted them back hard against the joints.

A roar of pain lifted from the blacksmith; he came off Kingdom in his wild effort to loose his thumbs. In the moment that he was free of Emilion's weight, Emilion straddling him, Kingdom wrapped his arms around the giant's legs and heaved upward with all his strength. Emilion's feet left the ground; he was lifted clear off it, arms thrashing helplessly. Kingdom came to his knees, still lifting, and then to his feet, Emilion's great weight held unbelievably helpless above him.

Then Kingdom dropped him. The blacksmith landed on his face. While he was still dazed. Kingdom came on to his back, hammerlocking Emilion's right arm up behind him. Emilion resisted it silently, and with all his strength, which was such that no ordinary man could have held him so. It was all

Kingdom could do to hold Emilion's wrist as far as the small of his back. But to the thickly corded thews of Emilion's huge arm, even this was uncomfortably painful . . .

'Enough,' grunted Emilion, his face in the ground.

Kingdom let go and came off him. There was a moment of awed silence around the fire. Emilion stood, shaking himself like a great mastiff. He gave his hand to Kingdom and powerfully wrung Kingdom's; his enthusiasm was boundless. 'The first time!' he roared. 'The first time!'

And Kingdom, about to remark that if Emilion had been twenty years younger, wisely concluded that Emilion would not take kindly to this.

Emilion looked about at the men, grinning hugely. '*Vive le roi,*' said Emilion DeLorme.

No one contradicted him.

The bets were paid and the talk died away as the men unrolled their suggans. Kingdom, carrying his bedroll off behind Sheep Dip's wagon, overheard Santerre accost Hassard over by the tailgate. Kingdom came to a dead stop and listened, their voices carrying through the fog.

'Kingdom is a top rider,' Santerre said, 'even a natural stud-horse man. Point would not be too good for him, green though he may be. Yet you make him eat the dust of the drag. Are you still taking out your petty revenge upon him?'

'Takes years of experience to make a top hand, don't give a damn how good he rides,' Hassard snapped. 'I reserve point for my top hands. Kingdom's raw, and he rides with the raw men.'

'If he will be of more advantage other than in the drag, place him there.'

'I'd send him away,' Hassard said coldly. 'Do you know how jayhawkers work? I do. They send a man into camp to size the situation off.' He told Santerre briefly of the incident at the chaparral where a rifle was fired at the posse when Kingdom had no rifle; obviously the man had friends . . .

'Anyone might have fired on you, you and the other drunken idiots in that mob,' snapped Santerre: 'Or you were so full of whiskey, you were seeing things. This is folly. Have no more of it.'

'Folly, sure. Who decided this fool drive to Kansas? Not you and not me—Kingdom.'

Villon's quiet voice broke in then: 'I pity you, Hassard.'

'What? Why you damn' lily-fingered snob! You pity me!'

'Yes, pity you,' Villon said, and Santerre's sharp reprimand of them both was lost on Kingdom as he walked on, head bowed, into the fog. He heard footsteps after him then, and turned to see a slim silhouette merge out of the milky haze.

'Kingdom?' a voice called. The word was followed by a raw racking cough that left no doubt of identity.

'Here,' Kingdom said, and came to a stop. Villon came up, blanket drawn around him.

'You heard it,' he said.

'Yes.'

'He is a damn cruel man, Hassard,' said Villon, an edge of anger to his voice.

'Doesn't matter.'

'You are charitable, Kingdom. Still, one day Hassard will make you truly angry. If he carries no gun then, I will name the corpse.'

'Thanks,' Kingdom said dryly.

The sick man turned away, back toward the fire, then stopped as though caught up by a thought. Villon turned back to Kingdom. He said levelly: 'A matter comes to my mind of which we should speak now, rather than let it run its course until harm is done.'

Wariness touched Kingdom. 'Yes?'

'I don't know whether my wife knows her own mind,' Villon went on evenly, 'but I fancy that you know yours well enough, Kingdom. I fancy that you know what you want—even if it should be another man's wife . . .'

Kingdom began to speak; Villon cut him off with a raised hand. 'Hear me out, Kingdom. It may be that you are playing a game with my wife which she may regret. However; I doubt that; I have taken your measure as that kind of man who can never be less than sincere. I wish to establish that to show you that your sincerity or lack of it makes no difference. I am appealing to your honor to stop the matter before it goes further.' He paused. 'To a point, I have been a blind fool. However—well, I was strolling by the house last night and on a still night, voices carry . . .'

Kingdom thought of last evening on the rear veranda; he chilled a little.

'I'm sorry,' Villon said in a wry way. 'Though I heard only one side of the talk . . . Mrs. Hassard, you will own, does not exercise the softest voice in the world . . .'

Kingdom said simply, 'I'm sorry.'

'No. Don't be sorry. Then you make me feel as though I am in the wrong to take this stand. And I do not think I am. I am only trying to keep my wife's name from tarnish . . . It may be that someday she will need someone—but, if so, you must wait till then.'

'I don't understand,' Kingdom said slowly.

Even in the fog then, he caught the strange ghost of a smile on Villon's mouth. 'It is in my mind, Kingdom, that I have come to this land to die . . . Good night.'

Kingdom, a frown deepening on his face, watched Villon vanish in the fog toward the wagons. Standing in the mist bound night, it came to Kingdom that all of them were like tornado-driven chaff, drawn into the vortex of something greater than they were.

CHAPTER FOURTEEN

Lute moved warily through the blackjack timber toward Santerre's camp. The night was utterly still; there was only the crunch of his boots as he passed the dreary, spectral march of trees in the cold mist. He moved to the very edge of the timber and paused there, hunkering down in the brush, straining his eyes to single out objects in the fog. Gradually he recognized the shadows pooling darkly on the ground around the dying fire as the forms of sleeping men.

His heart was pounding; his breath caught at his throat as he heard the sound of horses moving invisibly toward the wagons far to his right. They came dimly into view, horsemen merging out of the mist as though part of it, dismounting by the wagons and uncoiling their riatas. In these first days on the trail, there was no offsaddling, no slipped bridle. Every man slept with his riata about his wrist, the end looped on the saddle horn.

Nighthawks, these, Lute thought. It was time for their relief. The men straggling into camp, ground-tied their horses and moved forward among the sleeping men, waking some. One bent over a man not five yards from where Lute crouched. The rider shook the sleeping man's shoulder. 'Kingdom.'

Kingdom! Lute thought—a stroke of luck finding the man he sought so easily . . .

'Time for your watch,' the rider said in a low voice.

Kingdom rolled out of his blankets. He had only to put on his hat and he was ready. The rider's cigarette glowed ruddy contrast to the unrelieved shades of variant gray in this fog-shrouded night.

'Still,' the rider murmured. 'Real still. I smell a storm. Bad one. And that.' he added wryly, softly, 'might be all we need to set them off.'

'How are they?' Kingdom asked.

'Skittish, some. Can make trouble maybe. No saying.'

The other reliefs had already stumbled sleep-drugged to their horses, stepping into their saddles and heading out toward the herd. Here was luck; it would give Lute the opportunity he needed to speak to Kingdom. He stood and moved soundlessly through the timber, paralleling Kingdom heading through the ground mist toward his horse. Kingdom had a hand on the horn, one foot in the stirrup, when Lute called his name softly.

Kingdom stiffened, turning, eyes straining at the blackjack.

'Me, Lute. Over here.'

Leading his horse, Kingdom moved carefully into the shelter of the grove, coming to stand before Lute.

'It'll be tonight,' Lute said flatly. When Kingdom didn't reply, Lute massaged his chin with a hand and said wryly, 'You won't like it.'

'It's too soon. First night on the trail.'

'Not what I meant,' Lute said irritably. 'Incham means to stampede the herd over Santerre's camp. Wreck the wagons and carry away the remuda—'

'And maybe kill a few men,' Kingdom said quietly. When Lute was silent, he gibed, 'What is it, Lute? Weak stomach?'

'Dammit, yes, if you must know,' Lute snapped. 'I've seen enough killing.'

'You're ambitious, Lute. There's the price for it. That's part of what you pay.'

'Incham's going up,' Lute said harshly, 'and I'm going with him.'

'You're going down with him, then.'

A sickness and a shame gorged up in Lute. Then, with a mildness that astonished Lute, Kingdom said: 'You won't go through with it, Lute. You know you won't.'

There was this sudden ease between them, the tension gone. Lute said bleakly, 'You're right. And neither will you.'

'No,' Kingdom admitted.

'What do we do, then?'

'What was my part supposed to be?'

'At midnight Incham means for you to take care of the nighthawks—the ones likely to be dangerous. Do it quiet. You get a gun on 'em, and cold-cock 'em. Signal us with a shot then;

162

we're waiting behind the herd. We make it noisy—start the herd moving over the camp.'

'This is too quick.'

'He don't trust you. He likes you, but he don't trust you.'

Kingdom said thoughtfully, 'Go back to Incham. Tell him it's set.'

'What'll you do?'

'Warn Santerre. Tell him all of it.'

'Lord. He'll likely shoot you.'

'He likely will,' Kingdom agreed dryly. 'He'll be warned though. He'll be ready. Have a care of yourself—it'll be hell out there.' He scrubbed a hand across his jaw; the stiff rasp of whiskers grated along Lute's surcharged nerves.

'Hell, why worry,' he said half angrily.

'The war's over, Lute,' Kingdom said wearily. 'I'm through fighting it. Believe that or don't.'

Lute argued silently with himself for a moment, then said, 'I'll believe it, Jim,' and extended his hand. 'About Doug—he never took part in the worst at Lawrence. Or Olathe, Paola, Shawneetown, or the other bad places.' He cleared his throat self-consciously. 'Neither did I.'

'I wouldn't have guessed you had, Lute. Thanks for that—about Doug. Be easier on his family.'

'Sure.'

'Funny,' Kingdom said musingly, 'I liked

163

Incham . . .'

'Ah, the business tonight,' Lute said quietly. 'Don't blame him. He's a husk. War burned out the best in him.'

'An empty man,' murmured Kingdom; 'but the I-don't give-a-damn way he's got to him— why, it's a pose.'

'He puts on quite an act,' Lute agreed dryly. 'But one thing he needs, always: to feel that he's best . . . He needs power and he needs to feel that he has it, and he won't stop for anything in his way . . . Like tonight.'

'Like Hassard,' Kingdom murmured.

'What?'

'Nothing . . . You'd better get back.'

'Right away . . . What about Tory? Sooner or later, you'll have to meet him.'

'Let it be later, then. See you, Lute.'

'I doubt it,' Lute said gloomily. 'Watch yourself.'

They shook hands and Lute turned, took a step, then looked back. 'Curious. Why tell Incham you were Doug?'

'Health.'

Lute considered that, nodded thoughtfully, and forced a grin. They parted then, Kingdom to find Santerre, and Lute to work back through the timber to where he had left his horse. He mounted and cut out of the timber, making a wide circle around the herd. He headed down into a meadowlike vale where the shapes of men and horses took form out of

164

the fog.

'You, Lute?' It was Incham's voice. Lute replied, and rode in, stirrup to stirrup with the leader. The fog gathered so thickly in the low vale that only dark outlines of men and not their features could be discerned.

'He knows his part,' Lute said.

'When's he on watch?'

'Right now.'

'We'd better get into position, then,' Incham said. 'Lute—you, Lampasas, Valdez, take the left flank of the herd. Tory, take right flank with Woodring, Tremaine, and Herschel. I'll take the rear with the rest. Lute'—Lute could imagine him smiling—'has grilled you on the details of your postions with military precision . . . You flankers will hear Kingdom's signal shot, but don't make any noise until we in the rear start the herd moving. Understand . . . ? You know your jobs. Any questions?'

'One, Mr. Incham.'

'Tory?'

'Why don't we all make it noisy at once?'

'The ones behind the herd will start it moving in a certain direction—toward Santerre's camp,' Incham said patiently. 'We don't want you on the flank messing it by shooting too. Your job is to keep the herd guided that way once we've got it moving. Any more questions?'

There were none, and the group split up

165

into three parties which moved in on three sides of the herd, disembodied wraiths in the mist, keeping well beyond the easy perception of Santerre's nighthawks. Distantly, dimly, by straining his eyes, Lute could barely distinguish the bulk of the herd, the guards circling it, riding in pairs, their soft and lonely crooning to the cattle carrying obscurely to his ears.

A tingling raced up and down Lute's spine, prickling the base of his neck. The blood pounded thickly at his temples. Kingdom would have warned Santerre by now; Santerre would be planning a counteraction against the raiders. He tried to think how that counteraction would go, and could not. He had to be careful, was all. Let Incham and the others watch their own necks. A man had to take the cards as they fell.

The crooning of the night riders had died away. Lute became attentive, every nerve straining for sound and sight; but the fog had thickened and even the outline of the herd was barely visible. He could no longer make out the riders; that meant that Santerre's counter offensive was in motion. He would pull his men in to make Incham think that Kingdom had taken care of them. Thank the Lord for the thickness of the fog. If Incham even suspected . . .

Lute stiffened. He could hear a vast movement out there in the herd, and he thought, Midnight. It is immemorial with cattle in herds that they come erect at midnight, step restlessly about, and again bed down. Of all the moments which a drive could bring, this was, Lute knew, one of the most dangerous: the moment when every night guard tenses to the restlessness of his wards, the moment when an untoward incident could break all hell loose . . .

So Incham had scheduled his attack as nearly as possible for midnight.

It would come any moment now . . .

Lute looked over his shoulder at his men, strung out behind him at loosely measured intervals, paralleling the body of the herd. 'Ready,' he called softly, and they began to move in slowly toward the herd. He could see the dark forms of Lampasas and the others moving in unison, and it was odd to think that before the night had finished, some, perhaps all, of them would be dead . . .

The signal shot fired by Kingdom—or one of Santerre's men—came suddenly. Lute heard the shots and shouting as Incham's party converged on the herd from behind. Somewhere out there a steer snorted in fear. There was a violent concentration of motion through the herd. As one it surged. Lute's Spencer was out of its boot; he shot into the air, and his men closed in at the flank of the suddenly onsurging cattle. He heard the heavy roar of Lampasas' ancient Sharps over the

167

tumult of sound. At the opposite flank, Tory's men were peppering the air with pistol and rifle, and their rebel cries reached even here. Lute's men had taken up the shouting. The flanking parties pulled alongside the herd, racing on fleet cow ponies that no steer could distance.

Lute could hear the outbreak of shooting from somewhere ahead—Santerre's men at the forefront of the herd, attempting to turn it away from the camp. It was the best they could hope to do now; it could only be diverted and not stopped, for in its momentum it must run itself out until it could be milled. Nor could the flankers guide it now; it was out of their hands. Give your horse the free rein; let him run.

And then, from ahead, riding to meet them, what Lute had been watching and waiting for—uncertain shadows in the fog, quickly taking the forms of horsemen—a half dozen of Santerre's men . . .

Lute twisted in his saddle and shouted a warning at his men which must have been lost in the flood tide of heaving backs and tossing, clicking horns and the thunder roll of twenty thousand hoofs.

Lute turned his horse before he could meet the Staghorn riders head on, turning off at right angles to the path of the herd, to freedom in the cover of the night. Then Santerre's men opened fire, their guns winks of rosefire in the gray obscurity. Glancing back, Lute saw Lampasas pitch from his saddle. Lute was stunned. Lampasas . . .

He lost sight of the others in the confusion.

Then Lute's horse crumpled under him, suddenly hit, and Lute flung himself sideways from the saddle, landed on his shoulder and side with a grunt, rolled over twice, came upright unhurt, and started running on foot. He had lost his rifle. The tumult was well behind him now. He was safe.

Then he looked back and knew that he was seen and that this was the showdown after all: one of the Santerre riders had cut out of the fog in pursuit of him.

He reached for his pistol on the run. His holster was empty; he must have lost it when he left his falling horse.

He put his head down and ran, hearing the sound of the horse bearing down on him. The cold mist was on his face; he felt his feet running, running beneath him. Good-by, California. More dreams. Good-by, Oregon. Funny, you thought you didn't care a damn about living, but when it came to it, you were an elemental animal groping wildly for life, and all you could do was run.

Every sobbing breath seared his chest; Lute thought as though in a dream, hearing the thundering hoofs almost on him, Why doesn't he shoot?

He looked back to see why, and he saw the

horse and rider towering blackly over him, and he saw the rider's arm lift, and there was a flash of bright bursting flame in his eyes. Something smashed him in the face and that was all.

CHAPTER FIFTEEN

Kingdom had had no difficulty with Santerre whose quick mind was receptive to the information he had to offer. A few swift questions, and Santerre roused out his sleeping men. In seconds, the men were mounted and ready, rifles in hand, their gear assembled and pitched in the wagons which were driven out of harm's way. Santerre snapped out his directions: wait for the raiders to close in, then hit them with half of his men. Hit them before they hit us, some said. Santerre overrode this; wait, he counselled, and possibly they could surprise the enemy. The stampede would come regardless of any preventive measures when shooting started.

Santerre split the men; half to hit the enemy, half to turn the stampede. Then he divided the first fifteen again, taking command of eight himself to attack the raiders on one flank of the herd, assigning the others to Emilion, who would hit those on the opposite flank.

Santerre had placed Kingdom under Hassard who would take the remaining men and attempt to divert and mill the stampede.

Kingdom was among those who pulled far ahead into the probable path of it. 'Watch it, men,' Hassard's voice carried to him. 'When that beef comes through, it won't stop for hell or high water. Get in front of it and it'll run over you like a river. Try to turn it from the flank . . .'

Kingdom heard and felt the throbbing ground-pulse of numberless hoofs before he saw the black mass of the herd grow out of the fog.

The Staghorn riders whooped and shot into the air. Hardly able to make out the cattle yet for distance, Kingdom was already awed by a sense of the irresistable force of this massed hurtling juggernaut. He saw too that he would be caught in the outfringe of the herd's passage unless he pulled his horse farther to the flank; recalling Hassard's warning, he reined quickly that way.

Then, a careless shot by a rider—Kingdom felt the smashing impact all through his left arm. For a stunned moment, he lost control of his horse; the animal turned toward the very head of the oncoming herd.

In a panic, Kingdom wrenched the horse's head to turn him back toward the flank, and in the violent movement the horse stumbled and pitched sideways, throwing Kingdom partly from the saddle. Kingdom might have held on, but he fell on his wounded arm, and in the blinding hot pain of it lost his seat wholly.

By the time he had reached his feet, his spooked horse was gone.

The millrace of steers drowned all other sound now, and Kingdom, in its direct path and helpless, did not hear the rider; he did not even see the rider until the horse was almost upon him.

The man motioned Kingdom up behind him. Kingdom tried to swing up, but his wounded arm would not take his weight; he could not do it one-handed. The rider dismounted impatiently, assisting Kingdom into the saddle, then swinging up behind him. And Kingdom saw in astonishment that it was Villon . . .

The stampede was almost upon them; it would reach them before they could get beyond danger if they attempted to cut out of the herd's path at right angles. Instead, Kingdom turned Villon's mount in the same direction the herd was running so that they traveled the route of the stampede, but well ahead of it. Gradually, then, Kingdom turned the horse's head toward the flank, hauling them out of danger slowly but with a broad margin of safety.

Kingdom jumped the horse high over some brush, and hitting the ground again the animal kept on with no break of pace.

But Villon was gone! Hanging tightly at Kingdom's back on the slippery rump of his horse, Villon must have been unseated by the jolting.

With a frantic hand to the rein, Kingdom hauled the horse up short. And even then, with a single backward glance, he knew that it was too late: Villon was swallowed and lost somewhere under the roar of hoofs . . .

Slack with pain and tiredness, Kingdom rode into camp. The wagons were drawn up a few yards from the fire; horses were ground-hitched close by, their heads low, sweat-frothed, thick-drawn breath sighing audibly from their lungs. Ten or a dozen riders sprawled around the fire where Sheep Dip had the coffee boiler going.

Santerre stood at the tailgate of Sheep Dip's wagon, the sleeve of his shirt torn open. The cook was tying up a flesh wound in the owner's forearm. Santerre looked up as Kingdom slid from his horse's back. There was no rancor in his face; he lifted the cup of inky, scalding brew he held in his good hand in pleasant salute.

'Ah, *mon ami*. You make twelve. I fear not to see some others.'

'You hit?' Sheep Dip asked as Kingdom stepped wearily over toward them.

'Yes.'

'Hurt bad?'

'No,' Kingdom lied, wanting to talk to

Santerre alone. Santerre, seeing this, waited till Sheep Dip was finished with his arm, then walked off a short way with Kingdom.

'Didn't have time before,' Kingdom said. 'You'll want to hear the rest of it.'

Santerre did not answer; he did not stop looking at Kingdom while he explained fully everything he could remember of the past week. 'If I hadn't said anything to Incham of Abilene, this would not have come about,' he concluded.

Santerre snorted. 'If not this way, then another way. What of that? What of this of tonight? You saved my herd, possibly the lives of many men, with your warning. As for the man Incham, you were forced into his association by circumstance. No other has heard what you have told me; no other shall. Let us lay the incident aside; it is ended.'

Kingdom shook his head impatiently. 'Not ended. You don't know Incham. We beat him tonight, and he can't take being made second best. He'll strike back any way, anyhow, he can.'

Santerre said slowly, his dark eyes searching Kingdom's face, 'With what may he strike back? We wiped out his band this night.'

'Not all. Some scattered into the fog. He'll round them up somehow—if a man can do it, he can.' He looked intently at Santerre. 'There's—there's another thing . . .'

Something in his face brought Santerre

alert.

'Villon,' Kingdom said. 'He's gone—fell into the path of the stampede.'

He saw the shock wash across Santerre's face, but before the owner could say a stunned word, a horseman rode out of the darkness. It was Murray Ambergard. He grinned at Kingdom as though relieved to see him all right.

'Mr. Santerre,' Murray said, 'Egan said to tell you the herd's stopped. We turned 'em and milled 'em ; you can't tell the lead steers from the drag now.'

'The men are all well?'

'Egan took a count. Everyone's there, 'cept Villon and Kingdom, and Kingdom's here.'

Santerre nodded wearily. 'And all mine are accounted for . . . I shall ride with you to where you're holding the herd.' And almost under his breath, Kingdom heard him add, 'Ah, Jean-Paul. Poor Jean-Paul. Never the land for him, this . . .' He set his jaw and headed for his horse.

'Wait a minute,' Kingdom said sharply.

Santerre turned back to him with an impatient gesture. 'Incham and his men will not strike again tonight. There is no need to worry of them.'

'Not here, no,' Kingdom said slowly. He was trying to think of something—what Incham's strange mind would carry him to next . . .

Impatiently, Santerre turned to his horse,

and in that moment the full horror of realization came to Kingdom; he caught Santerre's arm and whirled him about as though he were a child.

'The ranch,' Kingdom said fiercely. 'The ranch!'

'What?'

'He won't hit here again. He knows we'll be ready. But one way or another, he knows he must get back at you. He'll ride back to your ranch and . . .'

'This is madness!' Santerre said. *'Folie!'*

'His, then. He runs to a pattern.'

Santerre shook his head incredulously. Rage beat high through Kingdom, hot wave on wave, a painful heart pulse in the fevered pain of his arm. He thought of Wanda at the ranch—she and Hassard's wife alone save for two half crippled crewmen Santerre had left behind.

A kind of madness came to Kingdom. Wordlessly, he turned and ran to his horse; his hand clamped on the saddle horn, and he swung up. He threw his weight on his bad arm and the pain nearly caused him to cry out. He kicked his horse around toward Santerre who stared up in amazement at this big, black-haired man with a bloody and useless arm from whose fevered and wild eyes every trace of brooding calm was suddenly gone. Kingdom had taken too much in these last days; his seemingly fathomless and passionless patience

176

had plumbed its last depth and had broken.

'Do I take it alone?' he asked harshly.

'Get down, Kingdom! You're sick!' Santerre took a careful step forward, then lunged suddenly for Kingdom's rein.

Kingdom reined the sorrel hard; the horse lunged in against Santerre, his shoulder hitting the rancher in the chest and staggering him.

With a violent hand, Kingdom turned the sorrel into the fog in a run that jolted his shoulder into a heightened crescendo of agony. He heard Santerre shout after him once and then the camp was behind him.

CHAPTER SIXTEEN

The fog had lifted and a fine drizzle had set in. Incham sat his horse at the summit of the rise overlooking Staghorn. His men—four in number now, including Tory Stark—were about him, their horses head-hung with exhaustion. Around them, the gray dawn, a less murky gray than the fog of the night, lifted silently.

Incham said, 'Come on.'

They rode down into the ranchyard.

A man on a crutch was limping out from the bunkhouse to meet them, quartering across to cut off their advance toward the main house. He carried a rifle. They pulled their horses up as he stopped before them.

'I know your bunch,' the man said. 'Get out.'

'Suppose you get out of our way, friend,' Tory said.

'Yeah,' the man said without moving.

Tory, with a single spare movement, shot the man down in his tracks before he could lift his gun. As the echoes of the shot died into the dismal dawn, Incham reined in his prancing horse and looked inscrutably at Tory. Tory was happy. He was very happy now. He slid a fresh load in his gun, his face full of soundless laughter.

Incham shook himself. He said irritably to his men, 'We'll see if there's anyone else in the bunkhouse . . .'

They found another crippled crewman, helpless on his back with a broken leg. Incham knocked Tory's gun up before he could shoot this man. Incham told Andre and Caples to take their horses to the corral, to rub them down, water and grain them, and tie them there in readiness. Incham and Tory and Delaney walked on to the house. Two women were waiting on the porch. One, Hassard's wife, had a rifle; the other, the small one, was holding a six shooter.

As Incham started up the short flight of steps to the veranda, Mrs. Hassard swung her rifle to train on him. Her face was pale, her hand steady. 'Are you feeling brave?' she

178

asked.

Incham halted, his foot on the top step, and looked at her. He said dispassionately, 'I'm taking over this house—for a while. I don't intend leaving until I'm good and damn ready. Keep your guns if you like, but keep the hell out of my way.'

Then he said he didn't want to be disturbed, walked on through the back door without another glance at any of them, and found himself in the kitchen. He started a fire in the stove, brewed up a pot of coffee, and sat at the table, drinking black coffee, and idly musing.

Now that he was here, he asked himself, why didn't he burn the place and get out? Santerre might fear something of the sort and send some men back ... But why should Santerre suspect?—he had no grounded reason to fear such. Unless Kingdom gave it to him. Whatever the case, Incham decided, he had a few hours' grace here while Santerre was too occupied in taking toll of any ravage of the stampede to worry of other things.

But all this was merely a sop for excuse in his own mind, Incham knew. He would delay the burning of Santerre's ranch as long as he dared, simply because he wished to sit here and savor the power of destruction which lay in his hands. In the next two or three hours, he could destroy or spare this ranch and no one could stop him. It was almost the very taste of deity ...

179

Once he had admitted this to himself, Incham felt better. He walked to the stove and refilled his coffee cup. As he set the pot down, a door opened behind him, the door of the corridor leading off the front room. Incham turned swiftly, defensively, some of the coffee spilling from the cup to scald his hand. He swore under his breath. It was Hassard's wife, he saw with a glance. She must have seen him spill the coffee; her face held a distant amusement. She carried the rifle in her right hand, the stock nestled in the crook of her elbow.

'May I have some coffee?' Mrs. Hassard said dryly.

'Go ahead,' Incham said irritably, slacking back into his chair at the table. 'And put that gun down. No one's going to hurt you.'

Mrs. Hassard leaned it against the wall, fetched a cup and poured it full, then carried it to the table, saying ironically, 'May I sit down?'

Incham's wise and sardonic-cynical eyes lifted to survey her for a long time. What the hell was she up to? 'Go ahead.'

Mrs. Hassard sank into a chair, sipped coffee for a moment, looked at the table and said nothing. He didn't encourage her. Finally she said, 'Would it be too much to ask who you are and what you want here?'

'It is,' Incham said shortly. 'It's none of your damn business.'

The remark did not disconcert her in the

180

least as he had suspected that it would not. Mrs. Hassard put her elbows on the table, crossing her arms. 'I think that it is.'

'You might be right,' Incham told her, rather liking her coolness. 'My name, then, is John Incham. Does that mean anything?'

'Incham?' Mrs. Hassard said thoughtfully. 'Oh, yes—you run a wild bunch of army deserters, don't you? Well ... what's the rest of it?'

Incham was nettled by the almost contemptuous note of her voice, but his admiration was mildly aroused. 'Last night I raided Santerre's market herd. But they were waiting for us ... The upshot of that is that I have four men left out of eleven.'

Inez sat erect, saying softly, her eyes on his face, 'Were any of Santerre's men hurt?'

'Ah,' Incham murmured. 'Worried about your no-good husband.'

'I am not worried about him,' Inez said dispassionately. 'I hate him.'

Incham smiled idly, searching his pockets for a cigar. 'You are a beautiful liar, my child, but a liar nevertheless.'

The woman looked down at her distended body and shuddered. 'I hate him,' she repeated.

Incham's agate eyes sharpened. 'Because you will bear his child? That is your mission in life.'

Her calmness broke. 'No! That's not so—

181

how can you say it? I know; you're like all men. A woman is for one thing, to be broken and used for that. What she wants or thinks does not matter.'

'If you believe that, you're a fool,' Incham said coldly. 'With any decent man, the happiness of his woman is first and last. Bearing his child is only part of it, and it her highest privilege as well as her greatest duty.'

Mrs. Hassard watched him, a pathetic note in a voice which had lost its distance, its contempt. 'Do you believe that? Really believe it?'

'I do.' Incham knew with surprise that this woman was asking him for assurance—the first time in her life, doubtlessly, that she had asked anyone for anything . . .

'You're an odd one, do you know?' Inez murmured. 'You don't fit your place in life, Incham . . . What happened?'

'The war mainly. Other things. Doesn't matter.' Incham dismissed this flatly and stood restlessly, walking to the window and staring out into the driving rain. Mrs. Hassard stood and came over to look too. A dark and rainpelted shape lay out there . . .

She said: 'You killed that man.'

'He was ready to shoot. It gave us some right.'

'That much?'

'Afraid?'

'You have that effect,' she murmured.

'He had his warning,' Incham said irritably. 'He was in my way.'

Mrs. Hassard said slowly, 'You're a sick man, Incham.'

'And you're a little fool. You're like all women; your mind is finite, limited. We come from dirt; dirt is our destiny. Why hang on to a thing like life anyway . . . ? Your hell is here on earth and of your own making. Probably did that fellow a favor. If I didn't what difference to him? We live our little egotistical span of years, they weep for us, then forget us. I say the hell with mankind and its petty inhibitions.'

Inez stared at him, startled by his bitter and scalding vehemence. Incham ended then, his eyes snapping into focus. Something was out there—something coming through the rain . . . A man on horseback rode ploddingly over the summit of the dune beyond the blacksmith shed. The horse did not seem to be guided by the man; it merely drifted slowly down toward the ranch. Incham saw now that the rider lay limply across the neck, his head bowed into the mane. The man had a death grip on the saddle horn with one hand, the other hanging limp, as though useless.

Incham flung his cigar away, threw the back door open, and sprinted out into the rain. He caught the horse's bridle and led him to the veranda, tying him to a wooden column supporting the roof, and turned his attention to the rider. He knew from the man's great

183

size, even before he caught a handful of thick black hair and turned his head to see his face, that it was Kingdom, his eyes glazed and nearly closed.

Incham saw the blood-saturated bandanna bound tightly above the triceps of his left arm and swore. He tugged at Kingdom's dead weight until it left the saddle. He tried to support it, but it was too much for his meager frame; Kingdom's whole weight came down limply into him. He slipped and fell with Kingdom on top of him. With a hard effort, he rolled Kingdom away and came up cursing, his face and clothes covered with mud. Inez stood in the doorway, hand braced against the doorjamb, staring. He snapped at her, 'Help me.'

They tried to pull Kingdom erect; his great weight was too much for a woman and a small man. Incham slapped him. 'You'll have to help us, Kingdom—hear me?' He slapped him again. 'Put your feet under you—push up.'

The last words must have come through to Kingdom; his legs straightened under him, and they could feel him lifting his weight though his head did not raise. His chin lolled loosely on his chest. They had only to support him on either side as he pushed himself erect.

'Walk,' Incham said. 'One foot after the other . . . That's it . . .'

They had some trouble getting up the steps; Incham cursed Kingdom until he lifted his feet laboriously up, one after the other.

They were in the shelter of the veranda now, out of the angle of downbeating rain, just as it began in earnest, slanting down in pale slashing sheets which churned the yard into a chocolate sea of mud.

'Where can we put him?' Incham shouted at Inez.

'My husband's room ...' She nodded toward the corridor leading off the kitchen.

Hassard's room was small and cramped and had a look of barren meagerness and hard, Spartan simplicity. They eased the big man down on the bare cornshuck mattress; Incham pulled his mackinaw off. Kingdom's clothes were damp from hours of fog and mist. Incham, seeing the gun in Kingdom's belt, took it.

'Boil some water,' he told Inez. He drew his pocket-knife and cut away the sleeve from the unconscious man's shoulder, then the blood-sodden bandanna bound around it. The cloth was dried on with the blood.

When Inez brought a basin of hot water and strips of clean material for bandaging, Incham soaked the fabric and blood away from the whole arm until the raw angry lips of the wound lay clean with fresh blood welling a livid trickle as fast as it could be washed away. The bullet had not gone through. From its angle, Incham judged that it had gone on into the bone and splintered it—perhaps lodged

185

there ... He shook his head. This would require a doctor's care. Little wonder that Kingdom had been nearly unconscious—doubtless with the pain of this as much as loss of blood.

Incham tied the wound up as best he could. Standing, then, he frowned down at Kingdom. Then he produced a cigar and lighted it, passively regarding Kingdom's still form through the pale curling smoke. 'Can you hear me, Kingdom?'

Kingdom's eyelids twitched and draggingly lifted, his eyes deeply recessed mirrors of obsidian. His gaunt and pain-ravaged face turned slowly to Incham.

'Hurt some?'

'What do you think?'

'Ha! Nothing much wrong with you,' Incham said, hesitating. He wanted to know for a certainty of Kingdom's perfidy, and yet he didn't. Why ask? Yes—why not fatalistically accept last night's fiasco as a bad cast of the gods of chance?

He started at Kingdom's sudden question: 'Where is she?'

Incham's gaze snapped into focus on his face with quick shrewdness. 'Where is who?'

Inez said quickly, 'They didn't hurt her, Kingdom. I'll fetch her ...'

Kingdom's great frame seemed to lose tension, as though in a sudden excess of relief.

'Well, well,' Incham said. 'Mrs. Villon, eh?

Why Kingdom! And you the idealizing moralist . . .!'

A wicked glint struck Kingdom's bright dark eyes in a sidelong glance at Incham.

'Still the moralist,' the leader observed cheerfully. 'Else you wouldn't get salty over it.' He stepped to the door, looked back, and grinned. 'Yes . . . I thought there was a reason you rode back here even if you were half dead in the saddle. I'm afraid my reputation has gotten considerably out of hand . . .'

Kingdom watched him silently, burningly. Incham grinned again and stepped out into the corridor. Mrs. Villon came hurrying down toward him, saying breathlessly, 'Is Kingdom—'

Incham pointed at the door with a tilt of his chin and she went in, closing the door after her.

Incham paced through the house like a caged beast. He found his men sitting in the front room. They already had the floor littered with cigarette butts; they looked keyed to hair trigger pitch.

Tory Stark came to his feet as Incham entered. 'I am an easy man, Mr. Incham, but not this easy. What are we doing here? When do we leave? This is no place for any of us.'

'Shut up,' Incham said absently, not looking at him, not looking at any of them. No one else said anything; they were too familiarly keyed to the occasional dangers of the leader's

187

shifting moods.

Incham stepped out onto the front veranda and started pacing, trying to come to a decision.

He must burn Staghorn to the ground immediately and clear out. He had reached the end of the veranda in his pacing and now he turned decisively back toward the front room—then stopped . . .

The room where Kingdom lay was at one of the front corners of the house; its single high window opened onto the veranda, and Incham started, then halted, as the voices of Kingdom and Mrs. Villon came suddenly to his ears. Only then he realized that the window of that room was about a foot above his head: the voices of its occupants came clearly to him—actually Incham stood no more than a yard from them with only the thick wall of hand-hewn timbers between.

'That's why I had to hire out to your father,' Kingdom said in a low voice. 'Incham thought me my outlaw brother. Best thing to do seemed to play along and wait for a chance to help your father . . .'

'It's all right. Please rest . . .'

'Your husband—sorry I had to be the one to tell you.'

'Go to sleep, Kingdom,' she said gently.

'Wait. It isn't the time, but there may never be another chance . . . I—I love you. That part didn't fit in. I—oh, damn it to hell!'

There was a flat hopelessness in his voice. No man of words, Kingdom, thought Incham wryly.

'Kingdom, Kingdom, you utter fool,' she said in a soft, strange voice. 'Can't you see it? Or won't you?'

Kingdom must have understood finally. Incham heard his soft curse.

Mrs. Villon said gently, 'I know, Jim. You're trying to hurt yourself now because you feel you're wronging the memory of Jean-Paul so soon after his death . . .'

Kingdom said miserably, 'That. Also he lost his life trying to save mine.'

'No. Jean-Paul was a dying man. His case was incurable—the doctor said so. Jean-Paul knew it, and so did I. Only it was a point of pride with him to pretend that it was not. But dying to save someone else—he'd hold that a fair exchange. Dying bravely and worthily—this was a matter of honor to Jean-Paul, and far preferable to the lingering death that was coming to him. Don't you see, Jim?—it's not dirty. It's what can give us strength, if anything.'

'But'—Kingdom struggled for words—'you take it so easily. Doesn't his death . . .' His voice trailed off.

'As the death of a friend. Maybe that sounds terrible, but it's only the truth. Jean-Paul and I—at the first—were in love with something in each other that never was. When we found out, we could only make the best of it . . . Jean-

Paul would never have consented to a divorce; he could not brook an admission of personal failure to the world. Perhaps that was a wrong kind of pride, but it was in keeping with the honor that caused him to save your life ... Jim, look at me. It was never a real marriage. Believe that.'

Incham stepped off a short way, to the edge of the veranda, staring into the rain and not seeing it and listening to the steady thrumming of the rain on the roof and not hearing it. It was a strange pleasure to know what the man and woman beyond the wall had found. He tried to remember how it had been with him once, and another, and he could call up only a dim sad memory.

Too full until now of his personal embitterments, he looked beyond himself with a new-found insight: he knew that he could not destroy this ranch—this home—and what it might mean to these people and their children to follow.

Incham stepped into the front room. Three of his men sat smoking. Tory was standing at the north window, hands rammed in his hip pockets, staring out at the drenched plain with his back to the others.

'On your feet,' Incham told them. 'We're leaving.'

Tory turned slowly from the window, the old mad devil dance of laughter in his dark eyes. 'Why, Mr. Incham, you waited too long, sir.'

Incham looked sharply at him. Tory was smiling delightedly; he nodded toward the window. Incham was at his side in a moment. He looked and saw nothing through the driving rain, then caught movement at the brow of the long slope which rolled gently down toward the outbuildings.

Santerre had come, and a rough twenty of his crew rode with him.

CHAPTER SEVENTEEN

It had begun to rain. Slowly at first; then the sky seemed torn from horizon to horizon. Hassard, gigging his horse after the others, put up his face to the rain, welcoming the beating and coldness and the wetness of it. The dawn was a dismal gray neutrality of storm-lashed wasteland and roiled murky clouds banked darkly over the land.

Hassard hunkered miserably into his saddle, shivering shoulders slouched against the slant of the rain, water runneling down in a tiny cataract before his face from the trough formed by the rolled brim of his hat.

This riding back to the ranch was another of Santerre's brainstorms. Santerre had been nervous and irritable for hours last night after the stampede. Hassard had attributed this to the after tension of the night's violence; but this morning, after stamping back and forth restlessly before the fire for a while, Santerre had turned suddenly, decisively, to his men and ordered them to saddle.

He'd left ten to stand watch over the herd and hold them at the spot; the remaining nineteen, including Hassard, he ordered to follow him and rode off without a word of explanation. All Hassard could tell was that they were heading on their backtrail, toward Staghorn.

Hassard, numb with weariness in body and mind alike, sat slack in the saddle, rolling loosely to the gait of the horse. He had himself started the turning of the cattle during the stampede. He had directed the rebunching of the herd. He had taken a cursory tally of their losses when it became light enough to see, riding ceaselessly to and fro throughout the night, expending the tremendous reservoir of nervous energy which lay untapped within him and which he had never fully plumbed.

The losses were small, in weak steers that went down, unable to hold the pace, to be tramped beneath their fellows. They found Villon—enough to recognize him. Hassard felt a wry disgust for himself, recalling his open contempt for the man. They found as well the bodies of three outlaws, shot down in Santerre's surprise counterattack. One of them Hassard had recognized with surprise as the short fat moonfaced fellow with whom he had played poker in Boundary not long ago and who had accused him—and rightly so—of bellystripping.

So suddenly that Hassard scarcely realized it, they were at the crest of the rise beyond which they could view the sprawling Staghorn house and outbuildings. Santerre did not even pause; he swung his arm, motioning them on, spurring his mount savagely into a run down the slope, the crew sweeping after him.

Then the shots crashed out from the house. Hassard pulled his horse up with the others. Santerre swung his arm again, directing them to cut off at right angles rather than ride into the teeth of gunfire. They headed in a body toward the wagon shed. Bullets kicked up the ground under them.

Hassard thought in bewilderment: The old man expected this. But how the hell?

They offsaddled at the shed, and at Santerre's direction took up positions behind fence and building. He commanded them to hold their fire; there were women in the house.

Hassard moved to Santerre's side behind the shelter of a wagon. 'What the hell is this?' he asked. 'Who're those fellows in the house? How'd you know they'd be there?'

'The ones that attacked us last night,' Santerre said grimly. 'Incham's men. Kingdom warned me that they would come to the Staghorn, perhaps to burn it in retaliation. He told me so last night. I did not believe him. Only a short while ago was I able to persuade myself that he was right.'

'How did Kingdom know?' Hassard asked, eyes narrowing. 'Was he with Incham? Where the hell is Kingdom, anyhow?'

'Never mind that,' Santerre said shortly. He stared through the steady rain at the house. 'Your wife and my daughter are in there with those men.'

'God!' Hassard looked wildly around as this bore fully home to him. 'I've got to get to the house . . .'

'Do not be a fool,' Santerre said sharply. 'You would be in the open all the way.'

Hassard whirled on a crewman at his side. 'Alf. Give me a hand. Lay a hold to this spring wagon.'

Santerre opened his mouth as though to speak, then closed it. He watched as Hassard and Alf tugged the wagon out away from the wagon shed. Hassard hauled it around to face the front of it toward the rear veranda of the house; then he found an old piece of rope and lashed the tongue down. There was a slight incline from the shed down to the house. Hassard judged that with a litle impetus the wagon could roll that far by itself. He climbed into it and flattened himself on the bed. He could depend on the low walls of the wagon as partial shelter from bullets.

He told Alf, 'Give it a push.'

'You are mad!' Santerre snapped. 'What can one man do down there?'

'Be all right once I'm up by the house,' said Hassard. 'Getting there's the hard part. Lend Alf a hand.'

Santerre shook his head, but he put his shoulder to the wagon with Alf, and they heaved together. Hassard felt the wheels stir creakingly, then fall into motion and roll, rocking and jolting, picking up speed on the gentle gradient. Through a crack in the front, his face pressed to the rough boards, Hassard could see the veranda pillar. With a mild scraping bump, it came to a sudden rest there.

Hassard lay on his belly, scarcely breathing, his Paterson in hand. The wagon had been seen from a rear window; the shot proved that. Whether they knew he was in it was another question. He had to get inside. He waited, watching the back door, every fiber of his body straining . . .

The door burst open suddenly; a man came out, lunging off the veranda not two yards past Hassard flattened on the wagon bed. He was making a break for the corrals, Hassard saw; must have left their horses there . . . Hassard lifted himself a foot or more, lining the Paterson on the man. But the fellow's back was to Hassard now; he swore and lowered his gun.

Then Santerre's men opened fire from the wagon shed. The jayhawker went down, sprawling headlong. He tried to struggle up, coming waveringly as far as one knee; then sighed as though in great weariness and slid

195

back on his face in the mud.

Hassard's attention swung back to the open door. Someone else going to make a break. A cold terror took him then. A big black-bearded man came through the door, gun in one hand, the other holding Inez—his wife—before him, her arm wrenched up behind her back, holding her helpless ...

Santerre's men could not shoot without endangering Inez. But Hassard was close and the big man hadn't seen him. If he could draw a bead from the side ...

The jayhawker edged across the veranda, slowed by his struggling hostage. When his right side was presented fully to Hassard's view, he raised himself again, laying the barrel of his gun along the top of the sideboard and drawing his aim with minute care.

The slight movement drew the man's attention; he swung, his gun blasting at the wagon. Inez wrenched free and threw herself down. A bullet smashed the top edge of the sideboard by Hassard's face, tearing off a foot-long splinter which flew away, the raw jagged wood hitting Hassard between the eyes, the pain blinding him. He squeezed off his shot and rolled flat against the wagon bed, claws of panic fixing in him.

Blood was running in his eyes, but he could see again. He was still and rigid for a moment, then realized unbelievingly that he was unhurt, and saw, raising his head again, that his one blind shot had found the mark. The jayhawker lay loosely spreadeagled on his back on the veranda, one arm trailing limply over the edge in the mud.

He saw Inez running toward the wagon then, and he came to his feet, caught her under the arms and swung her up into the wagon, pulling her down flat within its shelter. A woman in a million. No hysterics; no incoherency. Only her body trembled a little against him. He shook her by the arms, looking at her face.

'All right?'

'You're not.'

'Nothing. Piece of wood hit me.'

They lay for a while in silence on the rain-sodden boards.

Inez said, the words seeming drawn at great length from her, 'What brought you back, husband mine?'

'You're my wife. Is that enough?' Hassard could feel the old constraint falling back between them, and he knew suddenly that he could not, must not, let this happen. 'It was like something screaming in me,' he said slowly. 'I wanted to break you and hurt you, but it was beyond me . . .'

'My fault,' she said almost inaudibly. 'I married you to get out of that gambling hell.'

'I knew it,' Hassard said. 'I took you out because I cared for you. I'd hoped—in time—' He ended it there.

Inez said nothing for a moment; then, gently: 'You weren't very patient.'

'Never been my way,' he said. 'Lower my horns and charge into it, that's my way. Always. I never thought—till awhile ago—that that could hurt other people. Hated myself for what I'd done to us both, and that's no good either . . . Forget that. You're free after this.'

Inez didn't move. 'Is that what you want?'

He looked up at the sky. The rain, slackening off now, streamed off his face. He said simply, 'Answer to that is, I'm here.'

'Egan—look at me.' He turned his head back to her, and it came to him that for the first time the hard and beautiful mask of the percentage girl was softened in all its lines and the woman was there. She said very clearly, 'I don't want to be free . . .'

Hassard looked at her intently. He said in new-dawning wonderment, 'What changed that?'

'A man—a little man named Incham . . . Don't talk. Hold me.'

CHAPTER EIGHTEEN

When Kingdom heard the shooting, he hauled himself painfully off the bed onto his feet, and motioned Wanda to a corner. Then he took a step that carried him behind the door.

198

dead in there, and one of his men is cold-cocked on the floor.'

'Then,' Santerre said slowly, 'there is one man still in the house . . .' He glanced at two of his men. 'Get the unconscious one of whom Kingdom spoke, tie him, bring him out.'

They left the house, Santerre waving his arm to the men who waited by the wagon shed, guns at the ready. 'It is finished,' he called, 'save for one man. Surround the house so that he cannot escape. But do not get too close.'

The rain had stopped. They slogged through the mud up to the shelter of the wagon shed. Hassard was there, his wife close beside him, and Kingdom knew that something had happened here, and, without knowing what, that it was good. Emilion was there; he boomed a welcome to them.

Hassard, somehow looking beaten and victorious at once, stepped over to Kingdom. 'Won't discourse on this. Say I admit I was wrong. Let it go there.'

Taking Hassard's hand, Kingdom felt the last burden of the past week lift ponderously from his shoulders. 'You had to take the hand that was dealt you.'

'But not like that,' Hassard said: 'You too, Mrs. Villon. My apologies.'

Shooting broke out down at the house; they all turned to look. Lovelace and Granger came running up the slope, Lovelace favoring a wounded arm. 'He wants Kingdom,' Granger said, out of breath.

'What?' Santerre said.

'Fellow in the house. He's barricaded himself in your room. We tried to get close to the window and he got Love, here. He yelled out to us he wants to see Kingdom. And you.'

Santerre glanced at Kingdom. 'Shall we go?'

They left their guns and side by side set off down the slope, past Santerre's men, crouching behind whatever cover they could find, stopping a hundred feet from the house.

'You wanted to talk,' Santerre called.

The man inside raised himself into plain view in the window, and Kingdom went cold.

It was Tory Stark . . .

'I have a word, Kingdom,' Tory called, smiling recklessly, utterly insentient to the odds against him.

'I'll hear you, Tory.'

'A deal,' Tory said. 'You hear me too, Mr. Santerre. If Kingdom meets me now, you won't have to lose a lot of men, which you sure as hell will if you try to rush the house.'

'And if Kingdom meets you?'

Tory's laughter pealed out bell-clear, tinkling chillingly. 'One of us will be killed. If me—then that's what you want, isn't it . . . ? If Kingdom—then you call off your dogs and let me ride out. Only I say this: I won't leave without I meet Kingdom first . . . What do you say?'

'I'll take it, Tory,' Kingdom said, not looking

at Santerre.

The rancher wheeled on him. 'More madness! You are no gunman. You will stand somewhat less chance than an icicle in hell.'

'More than me to think of,' Kingdom said quietly, and Santerre was silent.

Tory said gleefully, 'I've been wondering if those yellow stripes on your pants are in the wrong place, Kingdom.'

'That's all, Tory. You'll pay the piper.'

'You'd better get a gun first,' Tory taunted. '. . . You should have stayed home, Yankee boy.'

They turned and headed back up the slope, his mocking quicksilver laughter floating after them.

'Why does he want you?' Santerre asked puzzledly.

'I shot his brother,' Kingdom said briefly.

'Ah—the stage incident of which I was told.'

They reached the shed. Santerre told the others of the proposal.

'Let me meet him,' Hassard said eagerly.

Kingdom said in an iron voice, 'It has to be this way.' He looked at Wanda's white face and looked away.

Hassard took off his gunbelt and handed it to Kingdom. 'Put that on and draw once.'

Kingdom did.

'Oh, Lord,' Hassard groaned softly. 'I seen running molasses that was faster . . . First of all, pull the damn belt higher. Never mind that low-slung business; it doesn't have to be hanging from your kneecaps.'

'Use two guns,' suggested Emilion. 'Twice as good chance, *hein*?'

'No,' Hassard said flatly. 'Hard enough to be accurate with one. Look here: bring your gun up natural. Take your time. You can't get your gun out first anyway, so take your time. Just remember that . . . Tory's hot-headed, and you killed his brother. He may get wild, shoot too fast . . . May give you your chance.' He measured Kingdom's size with a gloomy eye. 'You can outlast him, for certain.'

Kingdom turned without a word to leave. Wanda blocked his path. He looked at her. 'Move aside, Wanda,' he said.

She did not move.

'It's no good,' he said gently. After a long moment, she stepped aside, and he would never forget her face then.

He walked on, every foot seeming a mile. Down the slope, past Santerre's men, starting across the stretch of mud-choked yard to the house.

In a fluid movement, Tory climbed over the window sill and dropped like a cat to the ground.

He was smiling. His coat was off, showing the black butt of the gun buckled at his left hip for a cross draw . . . He began walking across the muddy yard.

Kingdom took three more steps, then drew

his gun. Tory's hand moved with the blinding sweep of heat lightning. His first shot was off before Kingdom could finish the movement of hand to gun he had begun before Tory had even moved.

Tory's shot was too hasty, a clean miss. It was as Hassard has said: facing his brother's killer, a temper mastered Tory, and his skill had left him. Kingdom's gun was out; it swung to a level. *Take your time.* Tory's second bullet smashed Kingdom's left shoulder only a little above the other wound.

Kingdom drew back a step; the Paterson, pointed low before him, went off in the pure reflex of this second numbing blow. The pain came then and for a moment he was blind with it.

When Kingdom could again see clearly, Tory was on his knees, sinking forward, his hands pressed to his belly. He was still smiling when he pitched on his face.

Kingdom turned; he walked blindly back toward the shed, thinking: It's finished. Really finished . . .

He got three yards. Two Staghorn riders, running to meet him, caught him as he fell.

*   *   *

'What a mess,' Dr. Flamsteed said cheerfully as he packed his bag. 'Two damndest subborn bullets I ever took out . . . You ought to rest

205

now, and since you damn well won't, here's your shirt.'

Kingdom swung himself off Hassard's cot and pulled on his shirt, buttoning it around the bandaged arm. It was late afternoon of the same day.

'Good of you to ride out from Boundary, Doc.'

'Thank that damn Hippocrates. Take it easy on that arm now.'

Kingdom said he would and followed the little doctor out to the front porch. Wanda was there, and her father, and the Hassards.

'What the hell you made of?' Hassard asked Kingdom. 'You're supposed to be dead to the world.'

'An ox is so tough, nothing but an ax drops him,' said Doc. 'How's the arm, Santerre?'

'No difficulty.'

'Good. So that's it.' Doc had just stepped off the veranda when Inez said faintly, 'I think I'm going to have a baby . . .'

'Oh, my God,' Hassard said. 'Doc!'

Hassard carried his wife into the house, followed by Wanda and Dr. Flamsteed, Doc muttering, 'Rest for the wicked—a hollow dream, dear friends . . .'

After a while, Wanda and Dr. Flamsteed came out. Wanda said happily, 'A girl.'

Flamsteed mopped his brow with a big silk handkerchief. 'My God,' he said. He set his black bag down, opened it, and pulled out a near-empty flask of J. H. Cutter. He drained it with a final pull and flung it away. 'You know,' he said conversationally, 'I think nature slipped. *We* do all the suffering.'

After Flamsteed had gone, Santerre turned to Wanda and Kingdom to look gravely from one to the other and to see what he had expected. This was the frontier, a land of quick death and of quickly accepted change, and Santerre took in without comment what he saw. It was right this time, it was good; and he had never had this feeling about his daughter and Villon.

'You will not feel Jean-Paul's death between you?' Santerre asked gently.

Kingdom looked at Wanda and she shook her head soberly.

Santerre smiled and nodded. To Kingdom, he said: 'So. A pat hand. Play it . . . *Sacre*! I have a drive to finish,' and left to gather his crew.

They stood in the dying light and he took her hand in his good one, but nothing more, because all this was too sudden. There was a strangeness to all of it that would pass.

'Look,' she said. 'The sun is showing at last.'

The golden warmth sped across the land to them, shadow sweeping away before it; it fell on them and held them. Watching, they knew that it would rain again. But the sun would be there, and that was enough.

More of our titles are available in Large Print.
Hardcover (and paperback) Press, G.K. Hall &
Co. titles that are not available at your
library can be bought from the publisher.

For information, transcripts, and
hardcover titles, please call or write:

Chivers Press Limited
Windsor Bridge Road
BATH BA2 3AX
England
Tel. (01 225) 335336

OR

G.K. Hall & Co.
P.O. Box 159
Thorndike, Maine 04986
U.S.A.
Tel. (800) 223 6121

All our Large Print titles are designed for
easy reading, and all our books are made to
last.